Dead Ahead

A Cape Cod Novel
by
R. Pease

Robert F. Pease

Flagg Mountain Press
13 Louisburg Sq.
Centerville, MA 02632

Copyright © 1994 by R. Pease

ISBN 0-9637154-1-0

Fourth Printing 1998

Prologue

The fog was so thick you could feel it against your palm if you moved a hand through the air. Against your face it was like webs clinging and pressing.

A Seaman was on the bow and we couldn't see him from the cabin. Visibility was down to almost zero.

For more than an hour the horn had been sounding. Had any other craft been on the water anywhere near us it would have heard and been warned.

There was no wind. The sea was flat calm, the light a gray murk.

A blip had appeared on the radar screen quite a bit earlier. As we moved nearer it seemed more and more likely that it was the Sea Bird. When we were close enough, and the coxwain had used the bull horn to announce that we were the Coast Guard, I had taken the mike and said, "Lisette? Michael? Are you there?" But there had been no answer.

"Two hundred feet now," said the radar man. "Dead ahead."

The coxwain set the motors in neutral. The engineer and I stepped forward onto the deck. We could just barely make out the form of the man on the bow. He had put out fenders to keep us from damaging the other craft when we came alongside. There was no sound except the faint hum of the radar transmitter and the soft wash of water along our hull subsiding as we lost headway.

Like a gray ghost the outline of the Sea Bird materialized before us. We bumped against her. It took only a glance to see that there was no living soul aboard. Slumped over the small outboard motor, however, was the body of a man whose head had been crushed. It wasn't Michael.

ROY

Six months earlier, the other end of the year, Michael came into my life.

Wind-driven snow was beginning to drift along the front of the house. I stood by the study window watching red cedars bend with each gust, a whirling whiteness obscuring the walk and the road and the edge of the pasture. Someone, head down but hatless, was coming along our street. A man. As he came nearer he looked up once. Did he see me standing there staring at him? I don't think so. His attention was on the mail box. Wet snow had accumulated on the side of it. I saw him brush it away with a bare hand and read my name there, Bartlett, and then come up the walk.

He must have stood at the front door for a long minute. I wondered why. In the cold and the seething snow, without hat or gloves, he should have been very uncomfortable, yet it was a long time before he pressed the buzzer once, firmly, and then waited.

I left the study and went down the hall and opened the door. Snow swirled into the vestibule. The sound of the wind was like the sound of surf on a sandy shore.

The man before me looked to be in his forties. He had a small bag in his right hand. His face was gray with cold, his eyes deep-set. He had large ears with detached lobes, and fine hair thinning and going gray at the temples. The summer coat he was wearing was his only protection from the storm and it was shabby with a button missing at the collar. He stared up at me from one step below. Thin blue lips parted and he said, "Hello, Father."

"I'm sorry," I said. "You're mistaken. I have no children."

He seemed not to have heard me. Perhaps, in the roar of the blizzard, my words had been lost to him.

"I would have known you even without the photograph" he said

"What photograph?"

"May I step inside?" he asked, as if I hadn't spoken.

Was he hard of hearing? I saw he was shaking with the cold. He looked sick. I was tempted to tell him to go back where he'd come from. At the same time, some deeper feeling left me troubled and undecided.

I took a step backward and he came into the entranceway. I shut the door. The abrupt quiet, the narrow confines of the vestibule, the silent appraisal we were giving each other, created a near unbearable tension.

"Take off your coat," I said, "and hang it up here."

He did as I asked and then followed me into the study.

We stood at opposite ends of the room, he, beside the old iron radiator and I under the painting grandfather left me of a four-masted ship in a hurricane, sails torn and waves boiling over her deck.

"You mentioned a photograph," I said.

Some color was coming back to his face, but his pants legs were soaked from the knee down and a puddle was forming where he stood. He rubbed his hands together, gazing around him at the wall of books behind my desk, the portrait of my great, great grandmother done by an itinerant painter more than a hundred years ago, the Victorian furnishings, the rug I had brought back from Afghanistan.

"They named me Michael," he said. "You could call me Michael, if you wish."

His voice was pitched in a middle register and there was the faintest hint of a brogue in it. As if he had sensed what was passing in my mind he added, "The family that raised me was Irish. Their name was Sullivan. They gave me their name. They saw that I got some education and learned a trade. They took the place of a mother and a father."

One of the rhododendrons outdoors thrashed against the glass in the rising wind as if to underline the note of reproval in Michael's voice. He had intended reproval. Imposter, he had to be, but he was going to play the role he had chosen to its limits. There was determination in his manner, and something calculated, too; planned, perhaps.

"I've known about you for eight years now," he said. "At first, I thought I'd never look you up. Why should I? You didn't even know I existed. And you surely didn't care."

"You're right about that much," I said.

He tipped his head sideways, his small, near-hidden eyes coming to rest on mine. "Of course I am," he said.

Had it not been for the storm, I would have been on my way to the airport that morning, and he wouldn't have found me at home. With my trip canceled I had time to kill, but I did not intend to let this person browbeat me for long.

"You were to have left for London this morning." he said, "but all flights out of Logan were canceled before dawn when they were certain this was going to be the big blizzard of the year. You see, I know a lot about you, Roy Bartlett, importer, buyer, Brewster native, scion of one of the older Cape Cod families. I counted on finding you here alone, thanks to the weather. I knew this would not be an easy interview, for either of us."

"You're beginning to irritate me," I said.

"Yes. I see that. I haven't been very clever about this. Maybe I've thought about it too long, let resentment build, instead of coming straight to you, the way any other child would have. Except that I'm not a child, though you're my father. I'm middle-aged now, and eight years ago I was not young either. You look young for your age. I'm old for mine."

"How old are you?" The question got past my lips before I knew why I was asking. Then I saw what it could mean and was already counting back.

"I'm forty-five years old, Father. I was born on January 19, 1943."

1943. My God! The war was on. I'd enlisted in '41. By January of '43 I was overseas. I was nineteen then. Cocky. Full of myself. A pilot. B-24's.

The spring before that, before going overseas, we were flying almost every day. Classes when we weren't in the air. A week-end pass now and then. Some of my buddies would get drunk. All the talk was about women. You'd think every officer in the Air Force only needed to snap his fingers and gorgeous bimbos by the dozens would lie down anytime, anyplace. It was all bullshit, of course. The ones that did make out usually had little to boast of - a stay in the VD ward later, as often as not.

Was I as obnoxious as the others? Probably. But I never had a lot of success with women. There was once, though, that last month before shipping out...

Michael was still staring into my eyes. He'd been following me, pursuing me down the years. Now he nodded. "You found it, didn't you," he said, and I could see in his face something dimly remembered.

What is it that makes people say they see resemblances? Yes, sometimes in photographs you can put the picture of a young man next to a snapshot of his father at the same age and see how they once looked strikingly the same. But to say a girl looks like her father, or a son like his mother, is pushing it pretty far. Still, there is skull shape, general complexion, stance, the color of the eyes. I was trying to remember the girl in that Texas town at the USO dance. What was her name? What was the name of the town? It was April. She was no older than I. Very fair. Her face wouldn't come back to me, and yet in the face of this middle-aged, malnourished male before me I thought I sensed something already known. Or was it only the power of suggestion? In an effort to recall the girl was I just looking for points of similarity?

"You gave her a photo of yourself," Michael said. "The two of you went into one of those photo booths near the field and had a picture taken. One of each. And you gave her the one of yourself because you thought it wasn't very good."

It was true. You put a quarter in a machine and stood in front of a camera - or was there a man there who clicked it off? It was a long time ago. But I remembered the brownish photo. It was terrible, I thought, and I did give it to her. And she gave me the one of her. We said we would keep them, and with them find each other again after the war was over. What became of that snapshot? In it she was smiling, looking left a little. She was gazing outward toward a life full of promise and adventure, a confident expectation of good things and happiness.

But I lost the photo. Forgot it. Never wrote the letters I promised to write.

"My mother still had the photo of you when I found her eight years ago," Michael said. He took a billfold from his pants pocket, got out a rectangle of once-glossy paper and handed it to me.

Outside the study, the rhododendron whipped the window as if it might break the glass. Snow was so thick in the air that I could no longer make out the fence posts across the street on the edge of the pasture.

And some of the storm's fury had got into the room. If this Michael Sullivan was my son he had not come here out of love, he had come seeking to settle an old score.

"Look at it," he said. "Take a good look into the mirror of your past and tell me what you see."

I scarcely dared to look, and yet I couldn't keep from doing so. My hand was shaking. I placed the photo on my desk and dropped my eyes to peer at it, felt the world turn on its side so that I could have rolled off its edge.

I've never kept albums of photographs, as many people do. There is no picture of me anywhere in this house. I had forgotten myself as thoroughly as I had forgotten the girl in the town in Texas.

But there I was, the nineteen-year-old, in the short-coat, recently commissioned, an even, bland, healthy, unmarked face, no real expression in the eyes. I could sense the emptiness, the unawareness of that other me, the total absence of any understanding of the harm I might do.

"She said the only reason she kept it was so that someday she could come after you for money."

I sank back into my chair. He was leaning on me. This was almost a physical attack. If he was my son, how come there was no hint of tenderness in his approach? And why did I feel nothing except discomfort in his presence?

I raised my eyes to look at him. He was shivering again. He was a pitiable figure in his shabby suit, water still running off his balding head, a clump of slushy ice fallen from cheap shoes at his feet. But he was glowering at me. There was hatred in his look, a lifetime of rancor he had nurtured. I could feel it and knew it could be justified and yet...

"You should get into a hot tub and then we'll find you some dry clothes," I said.

He stepped back as if I had struck him. Kindness was not what he had come for.

He spent more than an hour in the bathroom, the one my wife and I share.

She was away this day, had gone to visit friends in Hingham the day before because she prefers not to be alone in our old house when I'm abroad. As it turned out, I was the one who would have been alone here, due to the storm.

We've been married only a little over a year. This is my first marriage. Lisette is twenty-six years younger than I, of French parents, very beautiful. I've wondered at the good fortune that brought us together.

Now, here was a child of mine - if he was indeed my child - dropped out of the blue like a bomb to blow everything sky high, perhaps, a son I had never known existed and who was older than my wife. What was he after? What were his plans?

I found a decent suit in an old garment bag. Michael was about my height, a bit thinner. Clothes I would probably never wear again would fit him, I thought. A pair of loafers, a shirt, socks, new underwear - when I had it all together I knocked on the bathroom door.

"Come in," he said. I opened the door. He was standing at the sink with a towel around his waist. There was less flesh on his body than I had expected. You could almost count his ribs. He had got out my shaving gear and was lathering up. The bathroom was a swamp - a dark ring around the tub, soggy clothes on the floor, one of our towels slung over the top of the toilet.

I set my bundle down on the clothes hamper. "Here are some dry things for you," I said. "When you're dressed, come down to the kitchen. I'll fix us something to eat."

He didn't thank me or say anything. I closed the door again and went downstairs.

Six days a week a lady who lives nearby comes in and does the cleaning. Lisette was accustomed to having servants where she grew up in Lyon, and she has been admirable in her management of this oversized, early-twentieth-century mansion. I don't like to have anyone else living in the house with us so we have different people who come in on appointed days to take care of the shopping, the housekeeping and the grounds. Lisette has organized this beautifully and all our employees like her. She has something of a *grande dame* manner which could have rubbed local Cape Codders the wrong way, but her French accent and her smiles of appreciation for work done as she wants it done have turned all those in her employ into adoring vassals. Of course, we pay them exorbitant wages, too.

Lisette is as tidy as a rosebud, and I keep my things in order also. The newcomer did not look to be neat or caring. This would be a source of trouble quickly, I suspected.

I found some chowder in the refrigerator, set it on the stove to warm up. There were muffins and grapes. This would be plenty for lunch. While I waited for Michael to appear, I fixed a drink for myself, then stood by the kitchen window watching the snow that was falling faster than ever, though the wind drove it almost horizontally past the cleared area between the house and the barn. Along hedgerows and behind buildings giant drifts would be forming, but they were invisible now. This was a classic white-out, something rare on the Cape. Not since '78 had we seen anything like it, and before that how many years had it been? "It never snows on the Cape," we liked to tell newcomers. There were winters when this was almost true.

Michael came through the door from the dining room. I turned to look at him. In my old clothes he was enough like me when I was younger to make me catch my breath. He had shown me the photo of myself at nineteen. Now here was another replica at forty-five - my own ghost in different guises pursuing me.

He saw the drink in my hand. "Would you like one?" I asked, lifting my glass.

"I don't drink," he said - cold, critical.

I'm not an emotional man, but there are things I feel deeply. This person could not be my son. I would have sensed it had he been my flesh and blood. There was a gulf between us. He, even more than I, was intent on maintaining it. But that was puzzling. If he was here to establish my paternity, and if his interest was money, then why was he keeping me at arm's length this way?

I ladled out the chowder, put the muffins in the toaster, and we sat down at the kitchen table. I finished my drink and had reached for a spoon when it crossed my mind that Michael might be accustomed to saying grace before eating.

"You must have been raised as a Catholic," I said.

He hadn't picked up his spoon yet. "And you?" he asked.

"The family was always Episcopalian. Mother and Father were quite religious. I haven't been in church, though, since they died, except to get married."

"You're not a believer?"

He was quizzing me when I had wanted to learn more about him. Maybe he saw how that might be interpreted. "Yes," he said, without waiting for my reply. "I was raised as a Catholic, but even when I was too small to know what was going on, all the mumbo-jumbo made me uneasy. As soon as I could, I began to question everything. The Sullivans were troubled by my attitude. Much of their reason for adopting me was based on their wish to deliver one more staunch Catholic to the church. I was a disappointment to them."

He picked up his spoon and began eating. He was hungry and ate quickly. We polished off the chowder and the muffins.

Michael ate most of the grapes. When everything was gone we pushed the plates aside and sat watching each other on opposite sides of the table, the wind outside a steady roar and shingles on the north wall lifting now and again and snapping back into place. There would be trees down in this gale if it kept up. Power lines would be going, too. I could hear a plow on the state road, a hundred yards away, but there would be no way in or out of my home until long after the storm was past.

"When did you first start looking for me?" I asked.

He was running his tongue over his teeth, sucking pieces of grape skin or clam out of cavities and interstices. His teeth had had little care during his forty-five years. He had the look of one who has never paid much attention to health or condition, and yet he was stringy and hard like some old fish hawk and his eyes were almost yellow with the same cold, gimlet intensity you see in the osprey.

"I've been looking for you ever since I was born," he said.

"Where were you born?"

"So here comes the inquisition, right Roy? Wouldn't you know that my father's name would be Roy? It means 'king,' you know. Does that make me a prince?"

"Michael," I said, and it was not easy to call him by his name, "we need to get our cards on the table. We need to be sure of where each of us stands. There are facts which must be established. I'm not about to just take your word for anything you happen to say."

He used a fingernail to dislodge something from a back molar. His insolence was intentional. If I had been certain he was my son I might have leaned across the table and given him the back of my hand. But of course I couldn't do that. It would have spoiled any chance we had of discussing anything rationally.

"Where were you born?" I asked again.

"In Texas," he said, "in a home run by The Sisters of Mercy, in a crossroads called Point Tartar. That's only a few miles from Laredo. It was a Catholic home for unwed mothers."

"And it was there that your mother gave you up for adoption?"

"And thought she would never lay eyes on me again." By the way he said it I knew that he had determined to find her, and had done so.

"What was your mother's name?" I asked.

"Don't you remember?"

I deserved his contempt, but put in the wrong, and caught, I wanted to deny it. "You tell me," I said.

"Her name was Arlene Lamm. L-A-M-M."

I closed my eyes, set my elbows on the table and covered my forehead with my hands. I could see her now. Arlene. Arlene Lamm. As pretty as a field of Texas poppies. Young and fresh. Not all that innocent, perhaps, I told myself. Or was she? What could I have known about it?

It was a Saturday afternoon dance. A bus took us to the hall and there were at least three soldiers for every girl there, and the ones that weren't as fat as a Polish sausage were as tall as a phone pole or so ugly you'd go blind if you looked at them twice. My buddies grabbed anything they could reach, but I turned away and went outside and there, walking up the path, was this girl with fine blond hair and a wonderful smile. I knew that if she got inside she'd be mobbed and I'd never see her again.

"You're just in time," I said.

"What do you mean?" she asked, but she was already laughing.

"You're just in time to be rescued from that hall full of beasts. Let's get away from here fast."

Had she been mauled about at other USO dances, or did she just naturally go for me? I don't know, but we walked away from the dance and never did go back.

Michael had been silent.

"You see," he said now. "I do have the answers."

"Are The Sisters of Mercy still there, in Point Tartar?"

"They probably are."

"You're not certain?"

"How could I be?"

"Have you gone there?"

"Never, after I was born."

"Then how did you hear of them?"

"My mother told me."

"When?"

"Eight years ago."

The refrigerator motor stopped running. Something about the way it cut out made me stop quizzing Michael. I looked at the electric clock on the shelf over the sink. The second hand was no longer moving. I stood up and flipped the switch on the overhead light. Nothing. We'd lost our power. That meant no more water pressure. No heat. No more cooking, unless I could use a fire in one of the fireplaces.

I went to the wall phone and dialed the police. The line was busy. I tried Com Electric. Same result. Everyone must be phoning. While I was at it, I dialed the Hingham number where Lisette was staying. It rang a dozen times and there was no answer. She was out somewhere. Her friends too. Maybe they were on the road. Traffic would be stalled all over the area where this blizzard was striking.

Lisette wouldn't panic, even if she were stuck somewhere. Even if she were alone. Still, I couldn't help being uneasy for her. She'd call me as soon as she could, no doubt, but how long would it be before the phone line went dead?

I sat down at the table again. "We're in for it," I said.

"No more electricity?"

"And no telling for how long. It will be getting cold in here in an hour or two. You got the last hot bath until power is restored. Don't flush any toilets or run any water. Whatever's in the lines is all we have and we'd better conserve it. Let's hope we get service back before pipes start freezing."

Michael didn't seem concerned. It wasn't his problem. The storm meant nothing to him. He had walked through it to get here, without noticing. Since he'd been in the house, he hadn't once looked out a window to observe the wild and frightening beauty of this winter tempest. He was single-minded and, because of that, something else. I thought, for the first time, that he might be dangerous.

"So you saw your mother eight years ago," I said. "Where was it?"

"In Atherton."

"Is that in Texas?"

"Southern Texas. Not too far from the border."

"Had you seen her before?"

"Never."

He wasn't going to volunteer any information. I'd have to ask a thousand questions to get any kind of picture of what that meeting had been like. And was he telling me the truth? How could I be sure anything he said was true?

"Did she recognize you?"

"No."

"What did you say to her?"

"I said, 'Hello, Mother.'"

"The same way you greeted me. What did she say to that?"

"She tried to close the door in my face."

"But you forced your way in."

"Not exactly."

"What did you do?"

"I told her I wasn't going to go away. She said she'd call the police. I said it would look pretty strange for a mother to be calling the cops to take away a child who had found her after thirty-seven years of searching."

"So she let you in."

"Yes."

"Does she own her own home?"

"She did."

"You mean she sold it? Or...she died?"

"She died."

"How?"

"In an automobile accident."

"When was that?"

"While I was visiting her."

Why did I suddenly suspect that he had killed her? He was staring straight at me. There was nothing in his gaze to show horror or regret or guilt. Those yellowish eyes held no emotion.

"Did she own a car?" I asked.

"In Texas, if you don't own a car, you can't go anyplace."

"Was she a good driver?"

"I wouldn't know."

"Do you drive?"

"Of course."

"How did the accident take place?"

"She was drunk. It was nighttime. She came to a curve by the river and just went straight over the edge into the water."

"So she drowned."

"That's what the police report said."

"Was that particular road familiar to her?"

"It was a road she had traveled countless times. She was on her way to buy some more cheap gin."

He was talking about his own mother - if he was telling the truth - and yet there was no more feeling in the way he spoke than if he'd been telling me the color of some old car he once owned.

"Had she become an alcoholic?"

"Apparently."

"Do you suppose that having you appear could have affected her?"

"What do you mean?"

"Did she commit suicide?"

"That's a possibility."

I sat there in my kitchen, the chill already beginning to creep nearer as the wind rose ever higher outside, and I tried to imagine what life could have been like for the girl I had known so briefly just one afternoon in Texas. I had too little to go on, though.

"Did Arlene ever marry?" I asked.

"She did."

"Was he there with her?"

"He was much older than she and he died in the seventies."

"Did she talk about him? Did she tell you anything about herself?"

"What is it, Father? You on a guilt trip? You want to know all the dreary details of the harm you did?"

He had crossed his arms and extended his legs, one ankle over the other. From the pale gray formica table top the white light of the storm was reflected up onto his face. The big ears and the long jaw and the thin, sharp nose all loomed before me like a mask in a Greek play, exaggerated, magnified.

"Yes," I said, "for whatever reason, or reasons, I want to know as many details as possible. For a few hours one afternoon, a long time ago, a girl named Arlene entered my life and we shared something to which I gave too little importance. Maybe you were conceived that afternoon. Maybe. I need to know everything you can tell me. What did Arlene Lamm tell you about herself?"

"You really want to whip yourself, don't you?"

"Cut it out," I said, raising my voice. "I don't know if you're a child of mine or not. You're a bloodless, heartless specimen I don't understand and feel no love for. Right now, I'd like to kick you out in the snow and forget you. But I know that I couldn't do that. Kick you out - yes. Forget you - I never would. So all right. I'm acutely aware of having done something wrong. And I walked away from it with never a backward glance. There is probably no way to atone for this kind of wrong. At the very least, though, I can carry the knowledge of it within me. If that's wanting to whip myself, then you're right. Now tell me what you know."

For a moment, in my anger, I had nearly lost control. Michael had drawn his feet up under him as if to prepare for an attack. Now he relaxed again. He started talking, at last. Maybe he had wanted the chance to throw everything at me, after all.

"I was with her for a week before the accident," he said. "Most of the time she was drunk and nearly incoherent. She talked about you, came back to that afternoon with you time after time and what she said wasn't nice to hear. 'Find 'em, feel 'em, fuck 'em and forget 'em,' she'd say, as if that were the soldier's credo and you the epitome of every low-life GI in the US Army."

I remembered hearing that line during barracks bull sessions. Often I'd turned away from some braggart who'd used it - the sexist attitude that women were only things and men were bigger and better men, the more women they'd put it to. But Arlene, according to Michael, had placed the same label on me. And hadn't I, too, boasted of that afternoon's pleasure, and then later let it slip out of memory as if it had been without importance or consequence?

"Did she tell you that she got pregnant because of just that one time she and I were together?"

"You'd like to think she was some kind of pushover, wouldn't you, some little slut who'd been screwing everything on the base so you couldn't have been the one to get her pregnant. Is that right, Father?"

"That could have been the case," I said.

"You can stop kidding yourself. She'd been away at school, a Catholic girls' school, practically a convent, no men anywhere, and it was her first day at home that she had the misfortune to run into you."

"How about after me? Maybe she had a dozen other lovers the same week, or month. What about dates?"

"Desperate, aren't you, Dad? Grabbing at straws. Let me reassure you. I wanted to be certain too. There's something you may have forgotten about that roll in the hay, or the grass. Think back. Did you get bitten by something that famous afternoon?"

He was right, and I had forgotten. Before I got back to the base I began itching. It was awful. Maybe that was one of the reasons I had for forgetting Arlene so easily. I nearly went mad with insect bites that were from chiggers - a Texas specialty.

"I thought so," Michael said, seeing the recollection of that agony on my face. "Arlene had to be hospitalized that same night. She was under sedation for several days and then some of the pustules got infected. She was out of circulation for more than six weeks, she said. I doubt if she felt inclined to lie down with anyone for a long time after that."

"Oh God," I said aloud. "And then she never heard from me again."

"But she had your photograph."

"And my name. Why didn't she get in touch with me?"

"I asked her that. She told me that when her father found out she was pregnant he swore he'd kill her, but her mother just wanted to avoid a scandal. They kept her out of sight. They made contact with The Sisters of Mercy. When her time came, she bore me and then gave me away."

When he said that, his voice dropped. I saw his fists tighten. This was the thing he couldn't forgive. For the first time, something in me was moved to reach out to him. He'd been an infant once, a baby, and the first thing that ever happened to him when he came into the world was to be thrown away, given up by his mother, not even known to his father, handed around from one person to another, perhaps by nuns resentful of pleasures denied to them, a child of 'sin.'

"I'm sorry, Michael," I said, and leaned forward to touch his arm, but he drew back.

"You should be," he said.

The thin gauze curtain at the window moved as wind came through some crack around the molding. I looked out at the giant elm on the corner of the lot. All the other elms were gone, victims of Dutch Elm disease. This one still remained, but it was infected. With the wind out of the northeast, if it went over in the storm it would crash straight into the kitchen where we were sitting. Through the flying snow I could see its upper branches swinging left, then right, and bowing, leaning toward us, bent down by the weight of sticky snow and ice and a gale that pressed against it with all the uncompromising determination of a tank coming up against a single sapling in its path.

"So after you were born, Arlene returned to Atherton."

"And found a job in an insurance office."

"What kind of job?"

"She was a supervisor, she said, in the claims section. Until she got fired."

"Why was she fired?"

"They found out she had an illegitimate child."

"People don't get fired for that." I said.

"This was more than forty years ago, in a small Texas town. A very moral Texas town."

"How did anyone find out?"

"Her father was a drunk. He must have told someone while he was smashed and that someone told someone else. The word got back to her employer."

"But then she married, you said."

"Some time after she lost her job a man named Halloway married her. She became Mrs. Halloway. He was a kind of prospector and had once located a vein of silver that made him rich. He was way older than she was but he had money - at least he let people think that. It was Halloway's house she was living in when I found her."

"Did they have any children?"

"If I understood rightly, he wasn't much good in that department. He was old. He died only a few years after they were married."

"And Arlene stayed on, living in his house? Alone?"

"She soon found company, in a bottle."

"You don't know that for sure."

"No, but she'd been dependent upon alcohol for a long time before I found her. That was obvious."

"She would have been about fifty-six, eight years ago. How did she look?"

"She was a mess. She had a big distended belly. Her hair was so thin you could see her grayish scalp through it. She smelled bad because she didn't wash often enough. She'd lost most of her teeth."

He spoke of her with contempt. I kept thinking there should have been affection there instead. Why had he gone to the trouble of seeking her out if he hadn't felt some gentler emotion? Why had he come looking for me, for that matter? Surely, once, he had wanted to be loved. Does the need to be loved unfulfilled wither and turn into something else?

"You found her ugly."

"She was disgusting."

"But you stayed with her for a week, you said. What for?"

"I wanted to find out everything I could about the two people who were my parents."

"Is that so terribly important for you?"

"What do you think?" he asked, and I honestly couldn't say.

I was uncomfortable in his presence. Was that only because I was aware of how wrong I had been? Or was it because in his attitude I could sense only resentment and enmity? I could not like him. It seemed impossible that I ever might. Even if he was my son.

Very slowly the wind swung around to due north and sometime in the night the big elm went down. It just grazed the corner of the house. I felt the earth tremble when it went over and heard a branch scrape against the shingles but didn't get out of bed. There was no need.

Michael and I had eaten cold cuts and cheese and apples at the end of the afternoon. We'd already put on sweaters and hats. When it got dark, I gave him one of the guest rooms that had its own bath. I found extra blankets. We went to bed. It was the only way to stay warm. The phone was dead by then.

I didn't go to sleep for a long time. Once, I thought I heard someone prowling about the house, but it may have been the wind shifting and causing the house to groan and settle, heavy timbers moving a millimeter and then sighing, like some old man in his bed in the night.

Not until morning did the gale let up. When it was light out, I summoned courage and left my warm bed and got dressed. The house was so cold I put on gloves and scarf, and a knitted cap and a parka. There was no sound from Michael's room, so I dug out my insulated boots and went outdoors to view the damage, if any, the elm had done. We'd been lucky. The tree would have flattened the northeast corner of the house if it had fallen before the wind shifted. As it was, only the shed, a kind of mud room, had suffered, its one window broken and the door blocked by parts of the tree.

A drift across the front of the house, on the south side, was six feet deep. Wind-sculptured snow lay in whorls and eddies and patterns of infinite variety all down the road and across the field.

I struggled through an average of two feet of hard-packed but mostly dry snow to get to the road where plows had cleared a way. In open places the snow had been swept away so that you could see black spears of grass, sharp spicules, sticking up through only inches of ice. But wherever a hedgerow, a wall, or a building had been in the path of the gale, drifts, like curling, frozen white waves, had built up behind the obstruction.

The temperature was around twenty and some wind still sent dustings of powder into the air to swirl and pile up yet deeper where already deepest. In the ploughed road, new drifts were beginning to form, lying across my way like markers, property lines, nature's signaling of boundaries.

I wanted to get to a phone, if possible, if all lines weren't down. It was a mile and a half to the village. My face was thoroughly chilled before I got there. But the walk warmed my body, and the icy, spectral beauty of the winter countryside made me glad to be one of the first to be out in it.

Just as I'd hoped, Charlie Wilcox had his variety store open. Two plows were parked out front. Charlie lived upstairs over his place of business and kept open all the hours he was awake, year 'round.

I stepped inside and stomped off some of the snow. The smell of fresh coffee was so good I could almost taste it. Two men, who must have been the plow drivers, were eating blueberry pancakes at the counter. They'd probably been driving all night and would have a full day ahead of them, too.

Charlie was back of the counter, leaning over the grill. He saw me in the mirror. "You ready for some of this, too, Roy?" he asked.

"Just as soon as I make a phone call," I said, "if the phone is working. Is it?"

"Try it and see," Charlie said. "It was out all last night, but Matt here says men were working on the lines when he came down the road a while ago."

I lifted the receiver on the pay phone and put in my dime and sure enough, I got a dial tone.

It was a long wait before I had an answer, but Lisette was the one who said Hello.

"Are you all right?" I asked.

"Somehow I knew it would be you," she said. "Your trip was canceled?"

"Yes. I hope I didn't wake the rest of the household."

"It won't matter if you did. I tried and tried to reach you yesterday evening, but I guess the phone wasn't working."

"I tried once to call you before the lines went down. Did you get stuck on the road somewhere?"

"We went up to Boston to see a movie and it took four hours to get back to Hingham."

"But you're all right."

"Of course. And you?"

"I'm fine. I'm calling from Charlie's. The phone in the house probably won't get hooked up again for a while. And we lost all power, so there's no heat, or water, or cooking."

"Could you come up here until things are fixed?"

"Lisette..."

"I hear something in your voice. It is..."

"Lisette, a man came to the house yesterday, a man in his forties. He's there now. I want to talk to you about him. This is something serious. We can't discuss it over the phone. As soon as the roads are clear, will you try to drive home? By afternoon the expressway should be open. Maybe we'll have the power back on by then, too."

"What's this all about?"

"I'll tell you when you get here. Don't worry. Drive carefully. But please come as soon as you can."

She said nothing for a long moment. I could imagine her sitting there in a silk nightdress, frowning, back straight, her dark auburn hair loose over her shoulders, lovely. From what I had said she might be wondering if someone had arrived out of her own past. Did she have things she had kept hidden from me? Even as I let the thought cross my mind, I knew that nothing would make any difference to me. But how would she feel about a grown son of mine appearing on the scene?

"I'll get dressed now and see about getting the car out of the driveway," she said.

"Thank you."

"Are you sure nothing's wrong?"

"Don't worry," I said. "Just come home."

"All right. I'll get there as soon as I can."

I replaced the phone. By the time I got back to the counter, Charlie had pancakes and coffee waiting for me. He'd heard everything I'd said but he didn't comment. The two drivers paid up and left.

Short rations the day before and the early morning walk in the cold made Charlie's food taste as good as anything I'd had in a long time.

"You ever sleep, Charlie?" I asked.

"Don't need much sleep at my age," he said. "Only got a few years left. Don't wanna waste 'em sleepin'."

"You'll be here long after the rest of us are gone."

"Could be," he said. Then he leaned on the counter in front of me. "Did you know there was a fellow in here yesterday morning asking about you?"

"What did he look like?" I asked

"Middle years, no hat or gloves. Big flappy ears. Hair beginning to go."

"He's at my home now," I said.

Charlie wasn't about to say anything to that. Then I could see he changed his mind. "It's none of my business, Roy," he said, "but I think you should know that that fellow made me uncomfortable. Don't ask me how. I can't tell you. Just something about him made me want to keep looking over my shoulder."

Four young people came through the door. They were cross country skiers and had left their gear stuck in the big pile of snow by the entrance. Charlie was busy with them for a while. I finished up and paid and went back outdoors to walk home.

The sun had risen. A brightness, so intense my eyes hurt, lay on the land. In a single night the earth had been transformed, given a pristine coverlet so clean and new and fitting that you could sense, for a moment, what a paradise this world must have been before there were cars and roads and shops and swarms of people everywhere.

A field on my right had not a single mark upon it. It was a contoured, gently molded surface. I was certain no human hand could ever bring into being anything as perfect as the simple lines just wind and snow can form.

For two hours, when I got back, I shoveled, clearing a path from the front door to the drive and getting as much snow as possible away from the front of the barn so that when the man came to plow out the driveway we'd be able to open the barn doors and get our cars in and out. Later in the week I'd hire someone to come with a chain saw and cut up the elm.

I worked slowly, pacing myself, enjoying the exercise, forgetting that when I was though I'd have no hot water to wash away the sweat and ease the ache of stiffening muscles which would begin as soon as I quit.

Michael appeared when I was nearly through. He didn't offer to help. He'd put on all the clothes he could find and was still shivering.

"If you want to warm up," I said, "take this shovel and clear away some more of the snow from the drive."

"No thanks," he said, his teeth chattering. He was staring at me. "You're in pretty good shape, aren't you," he said.

"I swim a lot in summer," I said. "I play some tennis. I make a point of walking as much as possible. How about you?"

He ignored my question. "I found a picture of your wife," he said. "Was it taken recently, or isn't she as young as she looks in the photo?"

So he'd gone into my bedroom, too. Well, I hadn't said he shouldn't.

"She's a great deal younger than I am," I said.

I wondered if he had found his way into her bedroom, too. Had he looked into our closets? Our bureau drawers? "Did they tell you I was married when you were asking about me in the village?"

That brought him up a bit. "I did ask about you," he said. "I told you I'd found out about the trip you had planned to London."

For a minute I had him on the defensive. Maybe I should have pressed my advantage and quizzed him about other things, but I let the chance go by. Besides, I could not escape the feeling that something was painfully wrong between us. If we were, in fact, father and son, why had we not yet embraced? Why were we still behaving as adversaries? Hadn't this younger man come to me seeking reassurance, a closeness that had been denied him? What kind of heartless person would I be should I increase the hurt he had lived with all these years?

"I walked in town earlier," I said, "and had breakfast. If you're hungry, it's only fifteen minutes each way. You know the way. Walking will warm you up, and Charlie's pancakes and hot coffee will make you feel like a million dollars."

"I found some juice in the kitchen," he said. "I don't need anything else for breakfast."

He turned around and went back into the house.

Where, for a moment, I had wanted to reach out to him, offer him something, I had met indifference only. He was like an enameled cannister, the lid forever painted shut, impersonal, contents sealed inside where no one would ever look again.

"Shit," I said out loud, and wondered at my own vehemence.

I'd been ready to quit and go back indoors. Instead, I trudged down to the entrance to the driveway and went to work on the mound of ice and snow the plows had put there. When Lisette arrived, she'd need to pull her vehicle off the main road, so I worked for another hour and made a place for the Blazer she bought this year which, as it turned out, was the right thing to be driving at a time like this.

My own car, a BMW, was inside the barn. I wouldn't be using it for a while - at least not until Spud Wilkins came and cleared the driveway.

The wind was rising now that the sun was high. Drifts continued to form and parts of the path I'd shoveled would be filling in. A plow came along and put another wall of snow where I'd just cleared a place for Lisette. You'd think those bastards could see how much work it took when all you had was a shovel. But their job was to keep the highways cleared. They couldn't make a detour around every drive and path they came to.

Ten minutes later I heard a motor approaching. It was Lisette. I stepped onto the road and gestured for her to charge through what was left of the plow's last deposit.

She's the kind of driver who can get behind the wheel of a truck or a sports car, a bus or a VW bug, and know just what the vehicle is able to do. When we go on trips together, she does the driving. Undoubtedly, there are race car drivers who have sharper instincts for road conditions and how to handle high speed, but I know no man who is more at home in a car than Lisette. She put the Blazer through what was left of the two-foot pile of plow scrapings and went just far enough into the new snow to get her car all the way off the road. She cut the engine and jumped out.

How I got lucky enough to meet a woman like Lisette and then talk her into marrying me is some kind of miracle. I'm vain enough to admit that she might have done worse, but I'm still a little afraid that I don't deserve to be so fortunate.

She was as fresh as if she had only gone down to the corner. There was even a clean smell of lavender soap around her when we kissed, whereas I was beginning to have muscles tightening all over my back and shoulders and was ready to sag down into a snowbank and just sit there.

"How are the roads?" I asked, while I still held her.

"Not too bad," she said. "There were some places where the snow had drifted pretty high. Some icy spots. It was fun."

Three hours of slithering and stalling that would have put the rest of us in a foul mood and she could call it just fun.

"What about you?"

I let my eyes travel over the windows of the house and back to her.

"You'll be meeting Michael in a few minutes," I said. "He's forty-five years old. If what he tells me is true, he's my son."

We were still holding each other, hands on waists, feet toe-to-toe. In the white light off the snowfield, her eyes were a sea-green and bore into me seeking understanding. "Is that possible?" she asked.

"Apparently it is."

"You had a love affair once, many years ago?"

"I was in the army. It was shortly before we went overseas. I spent a few hours, one afternoon, with a girl whom I had almost completely forgotten. Michael claims he is the result of that encounter."

"What sort of person was this girl?"

"I hardly know," I said. "I didn't take the trouble to find out. I didn't even think about it. I was a dumb, conceited, ignorant kid. I took what I could. Then I walked away."

"She may have had contact with several other men at that time, if she was that...*légère*...with you."

"That's what I may have thought at the time, if I did any thinking at all, but I doubt it now that I've spoken with Michael. Perhaps it would be well for me not to tell you too much about it, or about what Michael has told me. That way you'll ask him your own questions and find out what you can and we can check with each other later."

"That seems a very cold way to deal with someone who may be your own child."

"I know it," I said, and some of the anger and frustration and confusion I was feeling must have been in my voice. "I know it, damn it, but Michael is not appealing or young or affectionate. You no more want to take him in your arms than you would an armful of slush from the roadway. He's remote. He's reptilian. He seems indifferent even though every move he makes has a look of being purposeful. I..."

"Don't get all upset over it. We'll find the answers." She leaned into me again and we held each other.

"This mustn't change anything between us," I said.

She didn't reply. How could things between us not be changed if Michael was proven to be my child?

From the beginning, almost as soon as we met, we told each other how much each wanted to have one child at least. For Lisette, nearing the age of menopause, after a career in the United Nations, having traveled widely and having done almost all the things she had once dreamed of doing, marriage and children had become an overwhelming need.

"There's a biological potential we need to realize," she once told me, "in order to have a complete life."

It was a rather chilly, analytical way of putting it, but it was something I felt too. I knew I had missed something essential by never taking part in the raising of a child. So we had done everything possible to bring about conception, but so far we'd had no success.

And here, like a boulder dropped off the side of a mountain, thudding to the ground at our feet, was a son I had never known, born and grown and grown old enough to look on us and judge us and question whatever we did.

"Let's go into the house and meet this new arrival," Lisette said. I saw her square her shoulders under her coat as she turned and preceded me through the drifts and up the walk I had shoveled to the door.

Michael was seated at the kitchen table with his back to the door through which we entered. He could have watched us through the kitchen window and then sat down when he saw us coming. He turned his head slowly and met Lisette's stare. I was struck by the way their eyes locked. You've seen prize fighters meet at the center of the ring when the referee gives them their instructions and they try to outglower each other, a mental contest of some sort even before the physical one begins. There was that kind of silent battle going on, I felt, or maybe it was only appraisal. I don't know.

Lisette stepped forward and held out her hand. "I'm happy to meet you, Michael," she said.

Michael got to his feet and took her hand. "Thank you," he said.

He was an inch or so taller than she, but it was evident that she was the stronger of the two, perhaps physically as well as mentally, and that must have troubled him. Did her beauty give him another reason for feeling inferior? Even bundled up in a sheepskin coat, with ski pants on and her glorious hair hidden under a thick plaid babushka, just her face was enough to set any man's pulse racing. I saw Michael take a deep breath and withdraw half a step.

What had been his relations with women? Was he married? Had he been married? I still knew next to nothing about him.

I've seen other men, meeting Lisette for the first time, step back and shake their heads as if to say - I give up, all I've known until now is nothing. But in Michael's expression there was something else. Was it pain? There was some of the hurt of an animal wounded but resigned, in the stiff unsmiling lines around his mouth.

Lisette, too, stepped back. "You have your father's sharp nose and strong jaw," she said. "Are you a shrewd business man too?"

"I don't know anything about business," he said.

"All the better," Lisette said. "One person to make money is enough in the family. Then the others can do important things."

Did a trace of a smile cross Michael's face?

"Well," said Lisette, looking around her. "I see that my kitchen is in quite a mess. Dolores has not come today, of course, and two men are quite helpless, even in normal times. So..."

And she put us both to work.

We were sent to the barn to bring in armloads of the wood which was stored there so we could get a big fire going in the living room fireplace. She got Michael to go through the debris in the back shed where the window was broken and find the hibachi we had used the summer before. Charcoal briquettes had to be somewhere, and sure enough, in the cellar, behind piles of old National Geographics and New Yorkers, we found - Michael was the one to spot them, in fact - two unopened bags.

"Water," she said next.

Like some magician, was she going to wave a wand and make it appear?

"Well?" She was looking at Michael and me.

"Well?" I repeated.

"We will need water for washing and cleaning."

"Everything is frozen."

She put her fists on her hips like some old-time fishmonger. "Is there not a new trash barrel in the barn?" she asked.

Michael and I exchanged a look. We'd seen it there and hadn't given it a thought.

"I will explain slowly," she said, "so you will both manage to understand."

But we had got the idea by them.

We went out into the cold again and got the new barrel. We filled it with snow and lugged it into the living room. There was just room enough on one side of the brick hearth so it could sit there by the blazing fire, the snow melting down and new buckets being added until we had a barrel of water all warm enough to be used for washing dishes later, and hands and faces.

We took a bucket to each of the toilets, too, so they could be flushed when we used them, and before all that was done, Lisette had the hibachi set up in a corner of the fireplace. Steaks from the freezer that had been thawing out with the current gone were hissing and popping there, filling the house with odors that made our stomachs rumble in anticipation.

When everything was ready, we sat around the fire, each with a porterhouse steak and bread with garlic butter on it. We drank the live red wine from Lisette's family estate in the country, a wine we bring back with us every time we travel to Europe and which has not been pasteurized or chemically treated so that once in a while it turns to vinegar. But when it is right, it's something authentic, nourishing, potent.

There was a whole gallon of tofuti in the freezer, too. It had to be eaten, or thrown away. We gorged. I think we finished three bottles of wine. We took our time and the short winter day faded. Darkness fell over the fields around us. We heard the plows once more and now and then a car. The wind had died.

Michael had said he didn't drink, but he tasted the wine and must have recognized its authenticity. He had at least two glasses of it and perhaps, because he was not accustomed to alcohol, it affected him so that he let us have glimpses of himself which later on we never saw again.

When Lisette asked him if he had eaten lots of steak in Texas, he said, "No. Mostly what we ate was hamburg. Mrs. Sullivan was not much of a cook."

"The Sullivans were the ones who adopted you?"

"Yes."

"They must have been...are they still alive?"

"They're both dead now."

"How long ago did they die?"

"Mr. Sullivan died when I was just out of high school. He was diabetic and they didn't know it. He passed out in the heat one day where he was working in the fields. They put him in a shed to recover. He was a farm hand all his life. When he didn't return to the field, they must have forgotten him. Later, when someone remembered, they found he had died."

"How dreadful. He could so easily have been alive still."

"He would have died anyway."

"Why do you say that?"

"He was overweight and he had terrible asthma."

"Maybe if they'd known about the diabetes they could have taken care of the other problems. Maybe they were caused by the diabetes."

"He wanted to die, though."

"Why?"

"Why do people want to die? I don't know. Some do. Sullivan was a failure. He was a nobody. He'd never done anything."

"He took you into his home. He and his wife took you in and raised you."

"He didn't do me any favors."

"Were they not kind to you?"

35

Michael seemed to think about it. "When they adopted me, they did it because they thought it was their duty - their Christian duty."

"They didn't have children of their own?"

"No. He was sterile."

"What about Mrs. Sullivan? What was she like?"

"She was just as fat as her husband. And just as ignorant. She never learned to read. When he died, she went to work in a mental health center - menial work. Cleaning."

"Did you call her Mother? Did you call him Father?"

"When I was little I did, but when I found out they had adopted me I switched and began calling them Mr. and Mrs Sullivan."

"That was rather strange, wasn't it?"

"I don't think so," Michael said. "They weren't my parents."

I had been leaning back, listening more with a third ear than with any conscious attempt to put together all he was saying. He managed to speak of the two people who had taken care of him through all of his formative years as if they were no more than two attendants at a clinic.

Surely the woman must have had some tender feelings for the baby she brought home with her. And how could the infant not have responded? Some bond between them must have existed once. I've held babies in my arms a few times. Can anything be more miraculous than a human child? Is there anything that fills one with wonder more than the look a baby gives you - that trust in you, no reservations, no suspicion? What would I not have given to hold Michael in my arms when he was born.

He sat between Lisette and me on a hassock, staring into the fire. He'd taken off the heavy sweater I'd given him and draped it over his upper body. The empty sleeves hung down almost to the floor because he was leaning forward, head sunk between his shoulders. Side view, like that, the dull orange light of the fire cast on his face, he seemed more a gargoyle than a man, some medieval monster carved in stone, until he turned and saw me staring.

"Does it disturb you, Father," he asked, "that you are forty-five years too late?"

I had to shake myself to find an answer. With Michael, again and again, I found myself rocketing back and forth between present and past.

"There's a lot I've missed out on," I said.

He turned back to the fire. "So have I," he said, and his voice had dropped almost to a whisper so that I was unsure if I had heard him correctly.

Lisette stood up and put another log on the embers before us. Sparks flew and bark crackled as it caught. Flames lit the room again and we all sat back away from the sudden heat.

"When did Mrs. Sullivan die?" Lisette asked.

Michael cleared his throat. "In '79," he said.

"Had she been ill?"

"She had a bad heart. All the extra weight didn't help. One of the neighbors went to see if she was all right when the mental health unit called to say she hadn't come to work. They said it looked as if she'd been trying to get up in the morning when her heart stopped. They found her half out of bed, one arm part way into her bathrobe."

"You weren't living there at the time?"

"I was in Brownwood."

"Is that a Texas town?"

"It's more of a city."

"You were living there? Working there?"

"Do you need to know all these things?"

"I'm sorry, Michael," Lisette said. "I don't mean to pry, but you've materialized out of nowhere and we need to place you, somehow."

"You mean you want to check out my story to be sure I'm not making it all up."

"If you don't want to tell us about yourself, you don't have to," I said.

Immediately, he stiffened.

"I have nothing to hide," he said. "I was a meter reader for the gas company. A real high-class job. I lived in a rooming house in Brownwood for nineteen years. The gas company gave me the use of a car. When Mrs. Sullivan died, I was notified and went back to Vision to settle her affairs."

"Vision is another Texas city?"

"Vision is a nothing town in the middle of nowhere. That's where I had to grow up. Until I was eighteen."

"Did you...did the Sullivans leave their property to you?"

"That would have been convenient. I quit my job thinking that would be the case. I got back to Vision and found Mrs. Sullivan's sister already there. Everything went to her - the house, the contents of the house, the savings account, even a life insurance policy for five thousand dollars. All I got was a sealed envelope."

He paused and looked from one of us to the other. "Don't you want to know what was in that envelope?"

"I think I can guess," I said, "but you better tell us."

"There was a single sheet of paper," Michael said. "Someone had written on it - 'Michael, your natural mother is Arlene Lamm of Atherton, Texas.'"

An hour later, we got into bed. The bedrooms were so cold our breath hung in a cloud before our faces, but we had heated bricks by the fire, and had wrapped them in newspaper and old towels and put them into our beds, two in Michael's bed and two more in the bed in my room.

"*Ce n'est pas une bouillotte,*" Lisette said, "*mais ça chauffe* - It's not a hot water bottle, but it warms."

With our feet on the bricks and our arms about each other we were soon warm again.

"I smell like an old horse," I said. There had been no way to wash adequately with only a bucket of hot water, washcloths and towels.

"Maybe a little strong," Lisette said, "but more like a goat than a horse."

She was warming her hands on me and touched me where there is always heat. "All that shoveling today has not made you too tired?"

"There's a smile in your voice," I said. "I can hear it."

"And so much wine has not relaxed you too much?"

"What do you think?"

"I think maybe this will be the night, if my calculations are exact."

A thick eiderdown from Strasbourg, which had once belonged to Lisette's grandmother, was over our heads. The temperature in the room must have been close to freezing, but under the covers, moving against each other, we were unaware of the chill.

"Hold yourself deep inside me," she said, and for a long time we lay together, fingers trailing lightly over the other's body, sensation everything, the world reduced to just the two of us.

We pulled the quilt back enough to breathe again. The moon had risen. Pale cold light filled the room. Lisette's lovely hair on the white pillow was ink-black and what I could glimpse of her shoulders was the color of old ivory. I longed to pull the covers all the way off us in order to look at her, to see us joined, but it was too cold in the room for that.

Unhurriedly we began moving again.

I have learned to wait for her. She knows when I'm waiting. It only increases my pleasure as long as she's not too slow in coming. She is sinuous and sensual. Her need, as she gets nearer, is all-consuming, voracious, a thing not to be denied. There are times when she's quieter, when she's passive and compliant, but when she starts to tremble, when she punches me in the sides, when her heels begin drumming on my back, then I must be there for her, let her use me, hold back until she's through crying out and shuddering and starts to go slack.

"Yes, now," she says then, and runs her fingers along my flanks and up the insides of my thighs, a touch as feathery and light as the wing of a moth, tantalizing, maddening, until I too have come and am spent and drained, and we roll onto our sides, facing each other, still locked together, sinking into the sweet oblivion of sleep after love.

But in those still moments, falling away into blackness, I was sure I heard a board creak in the corridor, and then another a bit farther down the hall. Had Michael stood outside our door in the piercing cold, barefoot perhaps, listening to us, spying on us? Lisette had already dropped off and I soon followed her, but what I had heard would come back to me. I'd remember it later on.

Sometime in the night, power was restored. I woke up soaked in perspiration. It was only just first light. I got out of bed and drew the eiderdown away from Lisette who slept on tranquilly.

How nice it was to be warm in the house once more, to walk around naked and not shiver. I went into our bathroom and found that everything still functioned. No water lines had burst in this part of the house.

A long hot shower was pure luxury, and by the time I was through there was enough light in the sky so the artificial lights were no longer necessary.

In the kitchen, too, both hot and cold lines were clear. We were lucky. I made coffee and toast and found butter and beach plum jelly and had breakfast. We'd have to throw away a few things that had lacked refrigeration for longer than was safe, but the meat in the freezer compartment could probably be saved if we used it soon, since it was only just finished defrosting.

I closed the damper to the chimney where we'd had the fire the night before and I checked the basement, but nothing was amiss down there. I was coming up the stairs when I heard a knock on the door. It was Spud Wilkins.

"You want me to do the drive, you'll have to move the Blazer," he said. A man of few words and humorless.

Lisette's keys were in her purse where she'd left it by the fireside. I put on coat and hat and went out and moved the

Blazer onto the highway. Spud had the driveway cleared in twenty minutes.

"Most snow we've had in over twenty years," he said.

I said it sure seemed like a lot to me. I paid him and he took off to do another dozen drives. He was going to earn the price of his new truck all in one or two days, by the looks of it, but he still wasn't going to crack a smile.

There was some clean-up shoveling to do to get the Blazer into the barn and I worked on the paths we needed which had been filled in by the wind the day before.

The air was sharp and clear. All around me the landscape was a sculptured marvel of sweeping lines, ridges and valleys, hollows and mounds. No one had tramped through the fields yet, or sullied the roadsides. Even the giant elm, which had come down so close to the house, lay in a bed of snow, its fractured stump covered and invisible, its broken limbs laid to rest, blanketed and sleeping.

By the time I got back into the house, Lisette was downstairs having her breakfast. When she finished, she followed me into my study. We kissed. On her lips was the taste of coffee. She smelled of pine soap and fresh strawberries. Where had they come from? Had there been some left in the freezer?

For a moment I was almost overcome with a need to tell her how much I loved her, but words that say this are inadequate. Deep feelings are better left shapeless but whole. We held each other gently for an extra minute and that said more than all the words one could put on a shelf lined with books.

I stepped to the door of the study and shut it. "Is Michael still sleeping?" I asked.

"As far as I know," she said. "He snores, you know. He practically rattles the windowpanes when he snores."

I hadn't heard that yet. The guest room, where I'd put him, is at the end of the hall and around a corner from my own bedroom. "Did you go to listen at his door?" I asked.

She nodded. "At first I wasn't sure he was all right. It's a fearful noise, but I guess it's just a normal sound for him to make."

"Did you know that he was listening at our door last night?"

"When we were..."

"Yes. When we were making love he must have been listening."

"*Tant pis pour lui,*" she said - "Too bad for him." But then she reconsidered her reaction and said, "*Pauvre type* - Poor guy." And after that, "He's a very unhappy person."

"Why do you say that?"

"Just watch him. For one thing, he doesn't know how to relax."

"I thought he was beginning to. He seemed more at ease last night when we were sitting around the fire."

"You need to look at his hands. They're always ticking at the arm of a chair, or his fists are clenched, or he's hugging himself. There's a tension in him which never goes away. He's like someone pushed to the edge of a cliff and trying to hang on to anything he can grab."

When Lisette first came to the States with me and we had only just been married, her English was already very good, but she had trouble with local accents and slang expressions. In a group, often, she couldn't follow all the conversations, but she could watch someone and later tell me things about that person I had never noticed or realized. What she had just said about Michael was something I might have sensed but would not have been able to express.

"Tell me," I asked. "Do you believe that Michael is my son?"

"I'm almost certain."

"Almost."

"So far, there's nothing in what he's said to make me doubt it. The problem is in the way he behaves."

"What about the way he behaves?"

"I don't know. Something's not right, not normal. I mean, a son should be seeking affection. Shouldn't he?"

"I've thought that too," I said. "But he's been short-changed. Maybe he's resentful. Or maybe because he's been deprived of the normal love of a father and a mother he hasn't learned how to love, or even to feel affection."

"He was listening to us outside the bedroom door last night, you say."

"I'm pretty sure that he was."

"This is a middle-aged man we're talking about. Maybe a child, an adolescent, would do that. But when someone the age of Michael goes snooping on people making love, there's something unhealthy about it."

"What would you like me to do about him?"

"That should be for you to decide."

"I don't like to think that he may be watching us and spying on us all the time. Suppose I set him up in an apartment somewhere else in the village?"

"You'd be putting him out, that way."

"Well, shouldn't he understand that we hadn't planned on having someone, a stranger, in a sense, move in with us permanently?"

"Don't you think you should find out what his plans are first?"

"I suppose so," I said. "You know, I still don't know anything about what kind of work he has ever done - except for reading gas meters in Brownwood, Texas. I wonder..."

"What?"

"I wonder if I shouldn't go out to Texas and do some checking up myself."

"Would you tell Michael you were going?"

"That's a sticky question, isn't it? If he is my child, but I don't trust his word, what kind of basis is there for any kind of relationship afterward? On the other hand, it would be naive just to take the word of someone I've never seen before without any proof. I don't know."

"And what about your trip to London?"

"That's only a matter of getting new plane reservations. As soon as the phone is working again I can take care of that. Unless you'd rather I put it off. You may not want to be left alone here with Michael."

"I can take care of myself," she said.

She didn't appreciate it when I was protective. Sometimes I forgot.

"With you away," she added, "he and I would have a chance to get to know each other better. He may be more inclined to talk openly with me when you're not here."

Probably that was true. Lisette has a gift for getting people to unburden themselves in her presence. Friends I've had for thirty years have told her things on first meeting her that they never told me.

"Then I'll reschedule the trip," I said, and later in the evening, when the phone was working again, I arranged for new reservations and then called my people in London about when to expect me this time.

I'd have to be gone for five days. That seemed a long time to leave Lisette alone in the house with Michael. But, of course, Dolores would be in and out doing the cleaning, and Lisette would be out some of the time, too. I was uneasy thinking about the two of them. We really didn't know anything about Michael, except what he had told us, and that might all be false, or just cleverly contrived. Not all of it. Some pieces fit. But if he was not the person he said he was and if he was up to something, five days would be more than enough time to do a lot of harm.

My work, from the beginning, was more a hobby than a necessary means of earning a living. I was stationed in England during the second World War and had a chance to see a bit of the country before coming home. I brought back a few things I'd bought there and was surprised to discover that some of them, here, were worth two or three times the purchase price in England.

My family, back then, insisted that I complete a law degree, once discharged, but after I got it, I took a trip back to Europe, and the recollection of how I'd picked up a few knickknacks, three years before, and how they had turned into much more money than they had cost, set me looking for other bargains.

It was like a treasure hunt. I found I had some special talent for nosing out items the American public craved but only European artisans could produce. I liked traveling around and poking into shops and talking with people who still worked with their hands.

That first summer, alone, abroad, was as exciting as any vacation I've ever had. And when I got back to Massachusetts, and the things I'd bought arrived, even after paying import duties and wrangling with officials and filling out untold reams of forms, I wound up with goods worth over twelve thousand dollars, while the summer's expenses, everything included, totaled less than three. And I'd had nothing but fun.

It took very little time to find the expensive shops where I could place goods on consignment. I soon had standing orders for any number of specialty items. My background in law was a help in finding a way through labyrinthian import regulations. Languages came easily to me. What was to stop me?

My father and mother were afraid it was a form of dilettantism at first, but I was soon making much more money than any fledgling lawyer and I was completely my own boss, free to go wherever the spirit willed at any time. I never did go into a law office. I've seen nearly every country in the world and the friends I've made are craftsmen and artisans, sculptors and painters, weavers and goldsmiths. The sordid clientele of the counselor-at-law has not been mine.

On this trip to London I was going to see a number of people who would be taking over representation for me, now that I was not willing to spend as much time away from home. There would be a small percentage of their gross which would come to me each year in return for a position already established and profitable. This was a business trip only. There would be no excursions into shops or studios. We'd be signing contracts, if all parties agreed to the terms. It was unlikely that there would be much to discuss because we'd worked out most of the details long ago.

The first day was taken up with travel. Flying east, if you depart in the morning, your day is shorter by several hours - five between Boston and London.

At eleven in the evening I phoned Lisette. She picked up the phone on the second ring. On the telephone she is still just a little bit awkward. It's the last obstacle when you're mastering a language. I've known foreigners who've been in the States all their lives. They speak fluently and without hesitation, even in a group, but when they answer the phone, they still mumble and stutter.

"Is everything all right?" I asked.

She answered, in French, that everything had gone well all day. "And you?"

"No problem. An easy flight. I'll have trouble sleeping tonight is all. It's only six o'clock for me now, but when it's my normal go-to-sleep time, I'll have to be ready to start a new day. And it'll be a busy one."

"Why don't you take a sleeping pill?"

"I'd rather catch a nap around noon. It's only one day that's difficult. What did you do all day?"

"Nothing very big." Now she was speaking English. "I cleaned out the fridge with Dolores, made a shopping list, took Michael with me to the supermarket."

"Was he any help?"

"You ask as if you didn't think he was."

"Well, was he?"

"To tell the truth, no."

"Why do you suppose he's this way?"

"Maybe he's just shy, or maybe he doesn't know how to be helpful."

"Where is he now?"

"Upstairs somewhere. In his room, I guess. "He's rearranged the room."

"Did he ask you if he could?"

"No."

"How did you find out?"

"Dolores went in there to clean up and told me afterward. She didn't say it, but I could tell that she wasn't happy about the extra work, and she did say he's very messy."

"He's going to cause us difficulties, I'm afraid."

"We must try to understand him, Roy. He's known some terrible loneliness."

"I suppose so, but I'm not going to let him make trouble for you and me."

I gave her my phone number and told her not to hesitate to call if she had any reason to want to. "I'll phone you again tomorrow at this same time," I said.

She said she'd be expecting it and hung up.

The next three days went quickly. I got all my business settled. By conservative estimate there would be two thousand dollars a month coming in just from the people I'd met in London. It would continue for ten years before ceasing and would be payable to Lisette for any unexpired portion of that term in the event of my death. By the time I made similar arrangements with all my other contacts there would be money and income enough to take care of Lisette, and the child we hoped to have, far into the future. There was already a considerable estate with which to provide for all of us.

Whenever I fly out of Logan I drive the BMW to Revere where a friend lets me leave it in his garage. I take a cab from his house to the airport. On my return to Logan, I caught a taxi to Revere and picked up my car. An hour and thirty minutes later I was home.

Lisette came out to meet me in the barn when she heard the motor. Was she a little less animated than usual? I thought I detected some hesitation in her manner. We embraced. "I've missed you," she said.

"Even five days apart seem long," I said. "Everything okay?"

She said things were fine and we went indoors.

There was a good smell of things cooking in the kitchen. I sniffed and looked at Lisette.

"Your favorite oyster casserole," she said, "and a green salad with everything in it except shellfish."

"And a drink beforehand?"

"Of course."

"I'll shower and change and be down in fifteen minutes. Where's Michael?"

"In the study, I think."

He hadn't come to meet me. I looked into the study. He was there. He was reading a book my father once gave me about shipwrecks in Cape Cod waters.

He glanced up. "Trip go all right?" he asked, noncommittal.

"No problems," I said.

For a moment neither of us seemed to know what to say next. Then Michael said, "You know, you really have the good life here, don't you?"

I wasn't sure what he meant by that. It sounded a bit like criticism.

"We're comfortable," I said.

"Yes. Quite," he said, and the way he pronounced the two words I could have been back in London.

There was a curious kind of confusion he created in me, a feeling of being in two places at once, in this instance; a feeling of living in two times, at others. Or was it simply Michael, this person come out of nowhere, real and unreal, a genie coiling up from the mouth of some forgotten bottle? Would he vanish someday, as suddenly as he had appeared?

"I'll be back down in a few minutes," I said, and went on up to shower and change. When I came back down Michael was still in the study and Lisette had joined him there with drinks for her and for me. Michael had set aside the book. I noticed that he wasn't going to put it back on the shelf where he'd found it.

"Tell us about London," Lisette said, after I'd tasted my drink.

"London's changing," I said. "I remember when I first used to go there, if you happened on a crowd gathered at an accident or where there was a brawl, there'd be a single Bobby at the scene with a night stick hanging from his belt and he'd say, 'Move it along now,' and the mob would disperse. Not anymore. There are demonstrations all over the place now and the police are there in force and can't always keep the situation from worsening. Maybe their presence even makes it worse."

"London's bridge is falling down," Michael said.

It was an appropriate comment, and surprising coming from him.

"Yes," I said, "in quite a real sense it is. There's a great deal of unrest and dissatisfaction. Much of London isn't safe anymore. You used to be able to stop anyone and ask your way, or how to find a certain shop or restaurant. Now, if you stop someone, or try to, they may draw back as if you are going to rob them. There are faces everywhere full of mistrust and downright evil."

"I'm sure you exaggerate," Lisette said.

"Or perhaps you're just getting old, Father."

"Some of the innocence of youth has worn thin," I said.

Lisette smiled. "I think you were never very innocent," she said.

"Oh but I was," I said, and I was thinking again about the mindless, bumbling, self-centered twenty-year-old I had once been, how I had understood almost nothing about the war I got into, or my part in it, or how I could affect the lives of others.

"I've never been in England," Michael said. "In fact, until I came here, I'd never been out of Texas."

"So this is like being in a foreign country for you."

"No, Lisette," he said, and I started at his use of her first name, but a second later asked myself how else he would be able to address her. "No, this is not much different from Texas. When I think of foreign countries I think of places where I wouldn't understand anything the people would say. I think of jungles or of arctic landscapes. I think of places that are strange."

Lisette was staring into his eyes as if to see what his real thoughts were. Was she simply studying him? I thought it was something more than that. Suppose she and I could not have a child, would Michael take the place of the son she wanted? But that was grotesque. He was seven years older than she. He couldn't be a substitute for a child. For a husband? That was a peculiar thought for me to have. Still, he was more of an age to be her husband than I was. I wondered. Had some understanding been established between them in my absence?

"Do you long to go to places that are strange?" Lisette asked him.

"Don't we all?" he countered.

He was slouched in his chair, legs extended before him, two fingers of his right hand tapping rhythmically on the leather arm of his chair.

"When I was quite young," Lisette said, "I used to fantasize about going away from home and living in a place where there were only children. But it was a happy place, and familiar. I never thought of it as unnatural."

"And then one day you crossed the ocean and came to live in this country. Isn't America quite a change for you?"

She turned to look at me, as if she should tell me something she had needed to say. "There are differences of custom," she said, "and of speech. There is a difference of culture. Many things are different, and at times I miss where I grew up. You don't escape from your heritage - if it's escape you want. Sometimes I feel a little displaced. But I'm happy here. Certainly nothing seems strange to me now."

Night had fallen and the last light had gone out of the sky. There was only black glass at the windows. The lamp, on my desk, shed a soft yellow powder of brightness around us.

"What used to make you think of foreign countries, Michael?" I asked.

He let his chin rest on his chest. "I used to think about going away from the Sullivans every day. I imagined walking south across Mexico and into the jungles of Central America where they could never find me and would never know where I had gone."

"Were they that unkind to you?"

"They were very strict. They had a thousand rules. If I disobeyed, or forgot something I was supposed to do, or didn't do something exactly the way they wanted it done, I was punished. They didn't beat me. It wasn't that kind of punishment. In fact, they never touched me. They sent me to my room and I had to stay there until they told me I could come out. I hated that room. I hated that tacky little house. I hated them."

His voice had dropped to a hoarse whisper. There was so much vehemence in it that I had the creepy feeling of some other presence in the room. Those Sullivans who had raised him could have been standing in the shadows behind me.

Lisette may have had the same feeling. She finished her drink and got up to pour us each another, looking through the doorway into the dining room and glancing into the corners before she sat down again.

"What about friends, playmates, school pals?" I asked. "Did you find other young people to play with while you were growing up?"

"I had no friends," he said. "There was one little boy who lived near us who used to come in to play when I was very young. But he went away."

"How come?"

"I don't know. One day he wasn't there anymore."

"Maybe the family moved away."

"No. The family was still there."

"What was his name?"

"I've tried to remember but somehow I can't. I was very young. I suppose memory is not as sharp at an early age."

That had not been my experience. I knew I could remember things from earliest childhood, but if I was asked to say what I had been doing a week ago, that was another matter.

"In school you certainly must have made friends."

"Did you?" he asked.

I had to stop and make an effort to remember. "There were some," I said. "Not too many, come to think of it. There was a real tough little guy named Paul Henry, when I was in grade school. We used to catch field mice in a shed in back of his house. We'd put a dab of peanut butter in a trap we'd made. The trap had a swinging door that only opened in. The mice would smell the peanut butter and push their way in through the door that was hinged with rubber bands at the top and then they couldn't get back out. We'd put them into jars with holes in the cap to let in some air and then we'd take them to school and turn them loose in the assembly hall or the bathrooms. We turned that school inside out a couple of times, before we got caught. Paul and I were friends for several years. I wonder what ever became of him?"

"You were lucky," Michael said. "Then, after grade school, you probably went to some fancy private school and rubbed shoulders with a lot of other rich kids."

There was that critical tone again. But he was right, except that at the academy I didn't like the roommate they assigned to me and I spent most of my time studying. Team sports didn't interest me so I played tennis and that didn't lead to any closeness with other students. Was I lonely? Maybe I was. Maybe a lot of kids are. But they don't know it because they have no doubts about themselves. I didn't. What about the ones, though, who don't feel secure, the ones who, for one reason or another, think they are inferior socially, or economically, or because of some stigma of race or parentage? Michael could have been one of those.

"Did anyone know that you were an adopted child?" I asked.

"Everyone did."

"How did they find out?"

"I told them."

"Had the Sullivans told you that you were adopted?"

"They didn't need to. I knew it."

"How?"

"I just did. All of a sudden one day I knew it."

"Do you know," Lisaette said, "that a great many children have this conviction even though it's untrue?"

"In my case it was true," Michael said. "And no one ever had to tell me."

"He wanted to be excluded," Lisette said.

We had got out the skis that were in the barn and were headed across the fields to the dunes and the beach. Very little of the snow had melted or evaporated in the week since the storm.

Lisette was an experienced skier. I'd tried it enough times to be able to get around moderately well. Going cross country, we had a whole new perspective on the places where I'd walked many times in the past. My sun glasses and the white contoured landscape made me feel I was seeing places I'd never seen before.

"Why do you say that?" I asked.

A pair of ducks came out of the creek at the base of the meadow. They were dark against the sky and the linings of their wings were pale and snow-lighted.

On our way we saw the tracks of small mammals, but the authors were not to be seen. Were they rabbits and raccoons, squirrels, maybe a fox?

Lisette paused on a rise. Her cheeks glowed with the cold and the exercise. I was breathing heavily but she wasn't. "He must have been aware of how he was different from the Sullivans starting at a very early age. It did something to him. I expect he felt superior. He wanted to keep it that way. I bet he put barriers between himself and others deliberately."

"Maybe because he wanted something they couldn't give him, he pretended that he didn't want it."

"This all happened when he was a very small boy. That would be a complex way for a child to reason."

"But it wouldn't have been reasoned," I said. "It would have been a way of compensating, something that came about without conscious intent and set a pattern of behavior which he couldn't change unless he found out and admitted that there was something he had wanted from those adoptive parents. But he would have forgotten that. It had never been articulated. It had only been an intuitive response when he was little more than an infant."

"You give an infant credit for extreme sensitivity."

"Why not? When there is less...or no language to get in the way, aren't instincts keener?"

"In any case, he closed himself off from others when he was quite young. I'm sure of that."

"I think you're right," I said, "and in a way it's made him an emotional cripple."

"Now that's going too far." She was indignant. I'd touched a spot that I should have avoided.

"He's not normal," I said, insisting even so. "A complete person has a complete range of emotional responses. He doesn't."

"You don't know him well enough to say that."

"Do you?" I asked.

"We had almost a week alone together while you were in London." She turned to look at me. "Are you a little bit jealous, Old Trader?"

It was a nickname she had given me when we first met and she made fun of me, as if I were some unscrupulous character from the old west, swapping valueless baubles for pelts with the Indians.

"Could be," I said. "He's a man, after all, and far younger than I."

"He's your son, Roy, and he's lived with a hurt all his life which we can scarcely begin to understand. It's made him aloof, and cold, and careful. But he's not some kind of mental case. If we listen to him, if we accept him as one of the family, his family, maybe in time he'll relax and find that completeness you've mentioned."

She'd decided to take up his cause. It was a part of her natural generosity, one of my reasons for loving her, and I would be wrong to oppose it.

But there were still a lot of unanswered questions. I was not as sure as she seemed to be that Michael was really my child. Too much in him was alien to me. He made me uncomfortable in ways I couldn't define. I was not actually jealous, not as I might have been of someone who could have come forward hoping to take Lisette away from me. It was more a fear that in siding with Michael, Lisette might not be enough on her guard. I didn't trust him. That was it. I still didn't have any idea what he was after.

We got to the edge of the water. A thin strip of sand extended along the upper half of the beach, but all the bay was filled with massive, jagged pieces of ice which the tides had broken and shifted. It was a vision of the arctic, bleak and frozen. The low yellow sun of mid-winter lay over it like a mist. Far off, we could hear the sound of gulls clamoring, but we couldn't see them. I wondered if this was the sort of arctic landscape Michael had imagined when he was a boy in Vision, Texas. Too bad he hadn't wanted to come with us.

We skied along the part of the beach above the high tide line where the snow was uneven. Then we cut across the dune to a beach road, for a while. No four-wheel drive vehicles had churned their way through it yet. They would, all too soon. Trees, along our way, had lost limbs. Many old trees had come down under the weight of snow and ice. Nature makes no special cases for the old or the sick or the infirm.

At the inlet, we had to turn back. We found a way across the property of others, through fields and over stone walls, back to our own place.

A dog had come out to bark at us once and had stood sunk in a drift up to his belly making a racket until someone called him back to his home.

We put the skis away in the barn and went into the house. I was tired, but it felt good to have used muscles that had not been exercised for a long time.

In the warm house we shed our extra clothes. Dolores had finished the cleaning. She served us lunch in our big kitchen before she left. Michael came downstairs to eat with us after Dolores had gone.

"I wish you'd been with us," I said.

"Where did you go?"

We told him.

"I'm not much of an outdoor type," he said.

We were eating a thick vegetable soup and had crackers and cheddar cheese to go with it. Oranges for dessert.

Lisette is a hearty eater. She never has to worry about putting on weight. After the exertion of the morning she was hungry and put away everything before her in record time. Perspiration beaded her upper lip. She is a woman of lusty appetites and makes no pretense about what pleases her - and what does not. She is sensitive to even the most elusive responses of others and is careful never to offend, but what she likes, she declares without inhibition. Her enthusiasm for things physical as well as intellectual is infectious.

I remember a time when six of us - two rather staid and proper couples plus ourselves - were in a club where a jazz combo was playing. A young man was on alto sax. He was very good and Lisette became so excited by his performance that even our four tablemates started to understand what was going on. I think they had some kind of hang-up about jazz, thought it was lower class, an inferior art form, but Lisette's exuberant delight in the music somehow opened their eyes (or their ears) and they realized that something spontaneous and remarkable was happening right there in our midst.

Michael was eating very slowly. None of Lisette's gusto had infected him. Well, he hadn't been out in the cold for two hours as we had so maybe he wasn't hungry - or maybe he didn't care for vegetable soup.

"You must have spent a lot of time outdoors in Texas," I said.

"Not all that much," he replied. "Summertime it's so hot you stay inside with the air-conditioning. In the cold months you stay inside to keep warm."

"Did the Sullivans have air-conditioning?"

"As a matter of fact, they didn't. But when I moved to Brownwood I had it there."

"You said you worked for the gas company. Did they have some kind of training program that you got into?"

"No. I saw an ad in the paper that they were hiring. I applied."

"Was that what the Sullivans had prepared you for?"

"Far from it. They made me take courses in farming. Mr. Sullivan was never anything but a hired hand. They thought they could make me into something better, as if raising soybeans, or feed, was a big step up the ladder."

"So you wanted a job with the gas company."

"I had to earn a living somehow. I wasn't going to go on living with the Sullivans."

"And you got hired?"

"Why not? I worked in one of the offices for a while, but when a meter reader took sick I asked for his job. It paid more and meant I had a company car. I kept that job for nineteen years."

"Why did you leave it?"

"Is all this important to you?" he asked.

"I'm still trying to find out what your life has been," I said. "What you've told us, so far, makes it seem pretty bleak. Where did you live in Brownwood? Did you rent an apartment? Did you make friends there? Have you ever been in love? Thought about marriage? I want to know who you are."

"You know who I am."

"I mean that I want to understand you and I can't if I don't know anything about where you've been for forty-five years, or what you've been doing, or what experiences you've had."

He pushed aside the unfinished bowl of soup and played with a cracker.

"I lived in a furnished room in Brownwood," he said. "I did a lot of reading. The people who owned the house accepted me the way I am. I got along with them. Often, they let me watch television with them in the evenings. I never missed a single day on my job. My boss at the gas company thought I was the best he'd ever had, but the girls in the office ridiculed me - said I was all business and no fun. I've never been in love, whatever that means, and I quit at the gas company, as I already told you, because Mrs. Sullivan died."

"Did you think she was going to leave what she owned to you?"

"Yes," he said, and he made it sound defiant, as if daring me to make something more of it. When I stayed quiet, he went on.

"She had promised she'd leave everything to me. I didn't know she had a sister or any living relative. I did know that somewhere among her things I'd find a birth certificate, or a paper of some sort, telling me who my real mother was."

"So you quit your job and went back to Vision and found out you wouldn't get a penny. That must have been a cruel disappointment."

Lisette touched his arm where it lay on the table. "But you were given your mother's name," she said. "At least you got that."

He went rigid when she touched him. Lisette's had been a simple, natural gesture, yet he caught his breath and tendons in his neck stood out until she withdrew her hand.

"Yes," he said. "I got my mother's name at last, and a partial address. I was finally able to track her down."

"**D**id you hear the way he phrased it?" I asked, when Michael had gone back upstairs.

Lisette was putting away the things we had used for lunch. "What?" she asked.

"He said, 'I was finally able to track her down.'"

"Is that so unusual?"

"It's the way you would talk about some varmint that had been ruining your garden."

"Roy, you are beginning to look for reasons to be critical. People don't have time to think about how every word they speak may be interpreted. I'm sure he meant nothing by it."

"I think it reveals his way of thinking."

She put the last plate into the dishwasher and straightened up. "I think that Michael needs to know that someone truly cares about him, cares for him. It seems that no one ever has. Or, at least, he's never felt that to be the case. Think what it must mean to a person, never to have been loved. Can you imagine that?"

"No, I can't," I said. "I doubt it ever happens. I've known some thoroughly unlovable people - ugly, mean, malodorous, crooked - and yet there was always someone who loved them, somewhere in their lives, but that didn't change them."

"Didn't it? Did you watch long enough to be sure?"

She believed in the goodness of most human beings. "There is an inner light," she once told me. I didn't want to contradict her. I half believe in it too. If you look for that light in others, and look hard enough, and believe it is there, then sometimes you will catch a glimmering of it. And someone like Lisette, with her intense faith in human decency, can set that light shining.

But I think the light can go out, too. In the very young it burns brightly, but as we grow older it becomes less luminous.

"If someone you know is injured, you will help him, or her, won't you?" She was close against me, those sea-green eyes only inches from mine.

"Of course," I said.

"You said Michael may be an emotional cripple. Well, maybe he's been injured emotionally. Let's try to help him. Let's try to give him something he hasn't had. I think his need is very great."

I kissed her lightly. "All right," I said. "Let's try."

Three days later, I had to drive to Amherst to see another person who was going to take over a part of my import business. I asked Michael to come along with me. He didn't want to go, but relented when I insisted.

We took off early in the morning. The temperature was in the low twenties. The sky was clear and the roads were in good condition.

I like driving, and the BMW is a joy to handle. Of course, in this country, you can't let it all out and really relish what a fine machine can do. In Europe, where I own a Mercedes, driving can be a challenge, even a sport. I've had that big 210 up to almost two hundred kilometers an hour a couple of times. That's something that gives you a sense of the precariousness of life. When, in one microsecond, you could be reduced to nothing but jelly, you live with a special intensity. It's a high, of a sort. I suppose that some drugs must produce the same exhilaration. Maybe not. The only ones I've tried, and that tentatively, have had the effect of removing me from life, putting me at a distance from it, lifting me above it into a dreamy euphoria where nothing really matters.

"Have you ever tried any drugs?" I asked Michael.

He was seated beside me rather stiffly. He'd fastened his seatbelt. I refuse to use mine. He turned to glower at me. "Whatever makes you ask a thing like that?"

"You seem to hold yourself very much under control," I said. "You don't drink. I just wondered if you ever let down your hair and completely relax. Drugs could do that for you."

"I've never been the least bit tempted to use any." He continued to stare at me. "Are you suggesting that I should?"

I smiled, "Hardly. It's just a question that popped into my head. What do you do to relax?"

"I'm not sure I know what you mean."

"I mean...do you have any hobbies? Are there sports you like? Games you like to play? You said you did a lot of reading. How about music? Do women interest you? Cars? Travel?"

"I'm able to get along without most of those things," he said.

He'd turned back to face the road. There was an emptiness in him which baffled me. I thought about what it could mean to be a meter reader for nineteen years. Did he think of anything else while on that job? Countless men and women have jobs like that where they do something automatically over and over, but their minds are on something else, aren't they? Don't they think about family, or getting laid, or going to a ball game or what they have to buy on the way home to fix for supper? Did Michael have anything in the back of his head which kept him moving from one day to the next?

There had been a determination to find out who were his parents. Had that been enough to sustain him for so many years? I just couldn't believe it.

We were on route 195 and there wasn't another car in sight. I thought I'd try something. We were going about sixty-five miles an hour.

Both hands on the wheel, I floored the accelerator. In seconds we were doing eighty, then eighty-five. I shot a glance at Michael. He was without expression. Ninety. There was a hint of a shimmy. At ninety-five it disappeared. We were flying. Far ahead I could see two cars which we would overtake quickly. I pushed our speed until it touched one hundred and then pulled my foot back and we were soon traveling at sixty-five again.

For a second, I think Michael's small, deep-set eyes had opened wide. Had I touched something in him? Was there a spark there? He didn't say anything. I never knew for sure, but I think he came out of himself for an instant. For a split second he hadn't been empty, wasn't in chains, obsessed. He'd been alive.

Perry Metcalf met us at the inn when we reached Amherst. He's in the Department of Romance Languages at the college and teaches a couple of courses in French Literature.

It was in Paris that he and I met. We were in a bookstore on the rue Vaugirard and both spotted a copy of Oscar Wilde's "An Ideal Husband" at the same time. I put my hand on it first and Perry said, "Son-of-a-bitch."

"I've been called that a few times," I said, "but Roy Bartlett suits me better."

Perry introduced himself. "Sorry," he said. "It's just that you've got longer arms."

He told me he collected first editions. He knew a lot more about old books than I did and had a pretty fair knowledge of what they were worth. I let him have the Oscar Wilde and we had lunch together - on him. It was the beginning of an enduring friendship.

Perry likes to spend his summers in France, but he's got four kids and his salary doesn't leave much extra for his hobby. I'd decided to let him take over some of my contacts there.

"Roy," he said, getting up from a big leather armchair, "you're good to come all the way out here."

We shook hands and he looked at Michael. "I want you to meet my son," I said. "Michael Sullivan."

Perry cocked his head. "You only got married less than two years ago," he said. "Gonna fill me in?"

We were both watching Michael. I thought I'd wait for him to answer the question. "My father never knew I existed until ten days ago," he said.

"Must have been quite a shock."

"It came as a surprise," I said.

"Where were you hiding all these years?" Perry asked.

"I wasn't hiding," Michael said. "My mother gave me up for adoption as soon as I was born."

"And after all this time, Bingo, up you pop. Wow! I hope nothing like this happens to me." Then he realized how that could sound. "But it's great, isn't it?" He looked back and forth from Michael to me. "You found each other. You've got a father, at last. And you, Roy, you've got a full grown son, and never had to change a diaper or get up in the night for a feeding. Some people have all the luck."

He had other questions, I could see, but he was going to keep them to himself until some later time.

We went into the dining room. Half the tables were empty. We took one to the side and had a leisurely lunch. Over coffee we took care of the paper work I'd brought along.

"This means a lot to me, Roy," Perry said. "I was gonna have to teach some summer courses next year in order to make ends meet. With this, I won't have to. You sure you want to let go?"

"I'm holding on to some of the biggest accounts for a little longer," I said. "I'll still be traveling some. But I'm ready to settle down at last and take it easy - a little easier, anyway. And you'll be sending me something each year I won't have to work for anymore."

"What about this son of yours, though? Have you thought about letting him take over some of your work?"

The odd thing was that until he mentioned it I never had.

"Michael," I said. "What about that? Do you think you might want to go into business?"

He hadn't said much while we were eating. He'd finished off some rare roast beef and scalloped potatoes and a dish of asparagus which must have been grown in Mexico. "I don't think so," he said.

"What do you plan on doing?"

"I'm not sure yet," he said. "I'm still adjusting to a whole new set of circumstances. I need time to think about it."

He added nothing more. Perry might have said something else, but I guess he was unsure of how much he should intervene. With four children of his own he probably knew plenty about handling this sort of situation. But Michael was actually older than Perry by several years, and there wasn't any genuine father-son relationship between Michael and me - not yet. This was an unknown quantity for Perry. It was for me, too.

When we went back outdoors and Perry had gone home, I suggested that we walk around the town and the campus for a while. Michael didn't protest.

The sky was overcast, but it wasn't as cold as I had found it earlier. Maybe the meal and the warmth of the inn had refueled me.

"You went to school here, didn't you?" Michael said.

"I had a year before going into service, then came back after the war and finished here."

"If I'd grown up under your care, I probably would have come here, too. Wouldn't I?"

He had spoken softly. It was like a voice within myself. A wave of regret washed over me. "I think you would have," I said.

I was on the point of putting an arm over his shoulders when I remembered what he'd said about his return to Vision after Mrs. Sullivan died, "I've been cheated everywhere I've ever turned."

"Michael," I said, and I stopped walking. He kept on for two or three paces before stopping and turning to face me. "Michael, I've done you a great wrong. I know it. I was young and stupid and unthinking. I wish there were some way to undo the harm I've caused, but there isn't anything anyone can do to change the past. So what we have now is the present and a little bit of the future. Can we make something of these?"

He didn't answer. I didn't know if I was getting through to him at all. Maybe the bitterness I'd thought was in his words had been imagined. Maybe he'd been expressing regret and I should have allowed my impulse to embrace him have its way. I think there were actually tears in my eyes.

"I'm in a position to give you almost anything you want," I said. "With Lisette and me you have a home now. Would you like to study? Men and women even older than you have gone back to school and earned degrees. We can arrange that, if it's something you want. What can I do for you? What would you like to do with your life and how can I help you to realize whatever aspirations you have? Tell me. Please."

A fine dusting of snow was beginning to fall. It was growing darker although it was only two in the afternoon. We'd walked onto the campus. He stood before me with the Chapel behind him. As an undergraduate I'd sat in that Chapel many times. The services, the hymns, the brief sermons - I remembered nothing of them. But I remembered Henry Mishkin playing the organ. I remembered the way he played a Toccata and Fugue of JS Bach and how it filled that chamber with the music and shook the building. It still echoed in me.

Michael hadn't heard what I did. I don't think he heard the thing I was trying to say to him, either. "I won't need your help, Roy," he said. "I'll manage by myself."

So cold, those words, like the wind coming across the valley and the new storm that would lock us in again. I should have known then I would never reach him, but I was too concerned with my own feelings of the moment, my wish to be able to offer something, anything, to make up in even the smallest way for what I had failed to give him before. But he was never going to let me make amends. He owed nothing to me.

We drove back to the Cape through a gathering blizzard. It took seven hours to get home and we only just made it. All roads were closed again before midnight.

Fortunately, we didn't lose power with that second storm. There was even more snow than the time before, though, and high winds caused drifting which, on top of the first snowfall, was impressive for Cape Cod. I couldn't remember ever having seen such a double whammy on the Cape.

Spud Wilkins came by and cleared the driveway again. "This keeps up," he said, "I'll reassemble the sleigh I got in the barn an' we'll all go for a ride to P'town." It was a long speech for him. He still wouldn't smile, but there was a kind of happy susurrus in his words, like the sound of new bills being rubbed together.

For a couple of weeks I was busy with paper work. I'd close myself into the study by ten in the morning and stay there until late in the afternoon, with just a sandwich for lunch.

Lisette was tied up too. She'd maintained contact with many of the people at the UN and was active in a campaign to reform that body. She was convinced, as were some others, that the International Court of Justice in the Hague had to be given the means to enforce its decisions. Simply to hand down an opinion which was binding upon no one, unless they found it advantageous, did little to settle any international dispute. There was to be a meeting in Brussels, later in the spring, of the people with whom Lisette was working. She expected to attend. There was plenty of work involved in making certain everyone got there, and in setting up a specific agenda with which all would be familiar before arrival. Just agreeing upon what to discuss was job enough.

I don't know what Michael did to occupy his time when Lisette and I were busy. I'd gone into his room once, when he was in the kitchen, wondering what it would tell me about him. There were soiled clothes on the floor, bureau drawers half open, the closet door ajar and things thrown in there or dropped. He had a small TV by his bedside. I know sometimes he watched that. A saucer and cup sat atop it with unfinished coffee in the cup. Paperback mysteries and newspapers were everywhere because when we were through with the day's papers he'd take them to his room. I'd discovered that he had an almost photographic memory for what he read. Several books from my own collection in the study had found their way to corners of his room.

He spent almost all his time in that room. He rarely went out, unless one of us insisted that he accompany us. Dolores had complained about his untidy ways. She couldn't stand it to have anything left in disorder, and each day, when Michael had lunch, she'd go to his room and set everything straight and the next day she'd have the same job to do over, not to mention the mess he left in the kitchen when he ate anything there.

Did he sit in his room brooding? Was there an interior life he led somewhere in the back of his head? What could it be?

I didn't think we should let him go on living this way, apparently without purpose or interest, and yet I didn't know how to approach him about finding something to do. He was like someone convalescent who needed a long time to mend, who shouldn't be pushed, whose condition was somehow precarious.

It was Lisette who first found something that appealed to him

When it turned warmer and rained and most of the snow was gone, she brought home a couple of magazines about sailing. They were on the kitchen table one noon on a Sunday when we were all three about to have lunch. Michael picked one up and began reading. He read it straight through and didn't take his eyes off it even while he was eating.

"Have you ever gone sailing, Michael?" Lisette asked, when he had finished.

He looked up at her but he was seeing something else. "Never," he said.

"I used to go sailing," Lisette said. "Summers, often, we went to Cap d'Antibes and friends there had a small sailboat. It was wonderful, except when the wind died."

"Is it something I could learn how to do?"

"Anyone can learn how to sail. To be very good at it takes a lot of practice, but you can have fun from the first day."

"Maybe I could get to be quite good. Would you teach me?"

"I'd love to," she said. "Roy doesn't care for sailing. I tried to get him to come along last year when we were invited on a trip to Nantucket in a real sailboat, a thirty-seven footer. He wouldn't come."

They both turned to look at me as if I were some kind of freak - a creature who didn't like to do something that they both knew to be exciting.

It was true. I couldn't see anything thrilling about being on the water in a tub that was at the mercy of the winds, tacking and zigzagging and taking forever to get anyplace. I've been lured out a couple of times and have found it exceedingly dull. Give me a craft with a powerful motor in it and maybe I'll go for a ride, if it's a hot day on land, but I have no love for open water. It's all the same wherever you look, unless it gets sloppy. Bad weather can come up fast and put any small craft in trouble, especially one that's entirely dependent upon the wind.

"I wouldn't have thought it," Michael said. "You're a landlubber, Father. All those sea-faring ancestors must be spinning in their graves."

He was curiously elated. He'd found something I didn't enjoy and that he might learn to do well. Was there a competitive angle to it? He and Lisette were aligned against me, it seemed. That lent some special zest to it for him. At first that irked me. Moments later, I realized that here was an opportunity for Michael to come out of his cocoon, to get into an activity with other people. He would be doing something, at last. Who could tell where that might lead?

"It'll be quite a while before you can get out on the water," I said.

"How long will it be, Lisette?"

She was smiling at him. She must have thought some of the same thoughts I had. "That depends on the weather," she said. "Also, we'll need a boat. We'll have to think about what we want. And what we can handle."

"It will be expensive, won't it?"

"How high can we go, Roy?" Lisette asked.

"Don't worry about it," I said. "As long as you get something that just the two of you can manage, there'll be no problem. If you start dreaming about something you can take around the world and that would need a crew, that will be another story."

There was a sparkle in Lisette's eyes when she turned back to face Michael. There was a new luster in his yellow-brown eyes, too. They were like a couple of kids who had just been told they could go to the circus and had enough money to buy all the popcorn and candy they wanted.

All through the slow Cape Cod spring they were busy with their project. They visited all the boat builders within thirty miles of us. They answered ads for Boats For Sale. They brought home books from the library and bought others in the stores. They acquired maps and marine charts and studied navigation and learned about compass compensation and fathometers and radio equipment.

Often, they talked to me about what they were doing. Other times, aware of my lack of enthusiasm for the sea, they huddled in the living room and I was excluded. That didn't bother me. For once, I was able to give both of them something that was making them happy. If now and then I felt uneasy about how they would fare when they started sailing, I put it aside. It would have been inexcusable had I said something to spoil their pleasure, or if I had started behaving like some old mother hen. They were full grown adults, after all. I had no right to insult them by cautioning them on dangers I had never encountered myself. They were going to be the experts. Not I. And they already knew more about being on the water than I ever would. Just the same, there were moments when I was troubled, and I couldn't say why it was.

The first week in April, I had to fly to Chicago for three days. When I came home there was a boat beside the barn.

Lisette came out to greet me. Michael followed. It was after dark and spring peepers were calling from the bog. The sky was clear. Enough moonlight fell around us so we could see each other without any lights on.

"We found what we needed," Lisette said.

I kissed her and held her. Michael came up beside us. I had still never embraced him, had not even taken his hand in mine, nor had he ever made any motion toward me.

"It's a Wianno Senior," Lisette said, "a twenty-five footer. It draws four feet of water and has an eighteen horse motor, outboard."

"We found it in Harwich," Michael said. "The owner used it just one season and then had a stroke. We got it for only half what it cost."

The hull loomed over us in the moonlight. It seemed very large. I knew that once put in the water and seen in the daytime it would not look as formidable, but standing almost under it in the dark I had the feeling it might fall upon us, which, of course, was absurd.

"Do you want to look it over?" Lisette asked.

There was a step ladder against the side of the boat.

"I think you'll be able to show me more in the morning," I said. "Can we wait until then?"

She was disappointed but didn't say so. "I suppose that makes more sense," she said. "And you must be tired and hungry now."

We went indoors.

I was glad to be home. I didn't like being away as much as I once had. Marriage to Lisette had given me a reason for wanting to stay at home. Besides, I've been every place I ever wanted to go by now. My father and his father lived in this big old three-story house all their lives. It's been home to three generations of Bartletts now. Perhaps a fourth would call it home too.

We sat around the kitchen table and I ate some rhubarb pie that had been left over from supper. I'd eaten a meal on the plane, but vanilla ice cream on top of the pie was too much to resist.

Lisette and Michael - Lisette mostly - told me how they'd seen an ad for their boat and hadn't dared believe it could be true. They'd phoned, first, and obtained the address. By good fortune no one else had answered the ad. They met the wife of the man who'd had the stroke. She blamed the boat for his misfortune, was convinced that if her husband hadn't overdone it, he'd still have been in good health. She couldn't wait to get rid of the boat.

The poor husband sat there in a wheel chair, unable to speak, his mouth trying to form words, one half of his body completely paralyzed. Lisette suspected that the boat had been his dream for half a lifetime. Probably the relief at getting away from his termagant wife had been so great, that first summer on the water, that when he had had to pull it out for the winter and go back to listening to her night and day, he'd burst a blood vessel in his brain and been turned into a helpless child.

"She was going to put him in his grave with that tongue of hers," Lisette said. "I didn't want to see it happen before our eyes so I got out the checkbook and we completed the purchase as quickly as we could. An hour later, we hired a man from East Dennis to bring the boat here. Now what we need to do is arrange for a mooring, probably at Sesuit. In only a couple more weeks we should be able to start sailing."

"If the boat is moored out on the water, how do you..."

"There's a tender at Sesuit that will take us out and back. We could use a dinghy, but there are the sails and other things to take on and off each time we go out. It'll be another expense, but not a big one. We've got the boat now and it's a beauty."

I was pleased to see how happy she was. If we were not going to be able to produce a child she would need other outlets for her boundless energy. I knew that she had been greatly disappointed when I told her how little I cared for sailing. Now, with Michael, she could spend as much time as she wished out on Cape Cod Bay during the summer months. He'd probably get to be a good sailor under her tutelage. Maybe he'd even learn something about order and organization.

If they didn't take too many chances, and got to be really proficient, there shouldn't be anything to worry about. I thought it would be a good thing for both of them to have an activity in which I did not participate. Even though I look forward to every hour I spend with Lisette, I know that it is being together after being apart which helps to keep our love fresh and new. Too much togetherness, too much of doing the same things together, could be like eating nothing but cake and ice cream - no matter how good it was, you'd tire of it eventually.

That's why I was glad, too, that she had the trip to Brussels coming up. She was going the next Wednesday for eight days and everything was ready for the trip. It would delay the first outing she and Michael could have until the weather was a little bit warmer. So much the better. A lot of commercial fishermen had been going out already, but the Bay waters were still too cold to be safe for anyone who got dropped into them. Sailboats, in amateur hands, can capsize all too easily. That raised a question in my mind.

"Michael," I asked. "Do you know how to swim?"

We were on our way upstairs to bed. I'd turned out all the lights on the lower level.

"Well enough," he answered.

"Where did you learn?"

"There was a lake near where we lived, in Texas. I went there often. It was one way to find relief from the heat."

"Did the Sullivans drive you there?"

"Sometimes. And when I was old enough to drive, they let me take the car if they didn't need it."

"What kind of car did they have?"

"It was a '45 Ford."

"Must have had a few miles on it by the time you were ready to drive."

"Over two hundred thousand," Michael said. "It used almost as much oil as gasoline. But it still ran."

We said Good Night to each other and he went down the corridor to his room. Every time we went to bed I was thankful that he had his own bathroom and didn't ever have to use the one Lisette and I share.

Lisette's bedroom is on the south side of the house and has another small room off it where she has a desk and takes care of her correspondence and the work with the Committee. We planned on making that room into a nursery, when the time came.

From the beginning, we'd decided to have separate bedrooms. She wanted to have one room that was entirely hers and could be arranged the way she wished. I'd been a little put out, at first, when she said everything in 'her' room had to go. It had been my mother's room and held many things which were important to me. We'd had to give some of them away and others were stored in the loft in the barn, but I understood how it could mean a great deal to Lisette to surround herself with her own belongings and to let her own personality dominate the room where she would spend more time than anyplace else. The results were startling and entirely satisfactory.

She'd had the floor sanded and given two coats of urethane. The old wallpaper had been removed, the surface made entirely smooth, and stencils had been applied where the walls met the ceiling. All the woodwork had been painted white. From her own home in Lyon she had brought a canopy bed, a bow-fronted dresser and an inlaid fall-front desk. An original Matisse was the only painting in the room. Saffron drapes enclosed the two windows. She liked fresh flowers and almost always had some on a small table by the bed.

I rarely sleep through the night. I wake up after three or four hours and like to turn on a light and read until I get sleepy again. Lisette always sleeps right through unless disturbed. That's why, many nights, I go to bed in her room so that we can be together, but later I get up and return to my own room.

That night I slept in the big canopy bed. The double hair mattress is at waist height. When I get old, and joints stiffen, I'll need a stool to get up to a level from which I'll be able to roll onto that surface. That should be several years into the future, however.

Lisette was waiting for me when I finished in the bathroom. She had the covers pulled up to her chin but she was naked beneath them. Slowly, I drew them away from her body. It's a moment we have learned to prolong, part of a ritual. She likes to see my delight in seeing her. She says she can feel my eyes walk along her body as I draw the covers down from her. We keep the light on on the bedside table, where there were jonquils that evening. It casts a soft ochre light over us and makes fuzzy shadows move around the room.

I sat cross-legged beside her on the bed and let my hands follow the path my eyes had taken. Is it an exaggeration to feel something akin to worship for the female form? It's no wonder that some of the most famous works of art in the world are of naked women. But how different from cold stone and flat canvas is living, sentient flesh. Where I touched her, Lisette pressed upward to fill my palms, nipples coming erect and hard, breasts warm and firm.

My hands moved along her rib cage and down her sides to the fullness of hips and flanks.

"Yes," she said, "look at me. Touch me lightly. Let your fingers dance on me."

My pleasure in doing all that gives her pleasure, in learning and re-learning all the shapes of her, only increases as time goes by. We are still finding new ways to maintain and prolong the excitement of love. The waiting, for me, for her to become fully aroused, is a time of intense visual and tactile delight, and when she begins to reach for me, playing with me, moving against me and with me, like an electrical charge I can sense a ringing in every cell of my body from my toe nails to each hair on my head.

She wanted to sit astride me that evening, to use me. She likes it when my hands are free and can travel all over her while she's moving above me.

She took me inside her then. Like a naiad she rode me, galloping, plunging, and moments later while she was still trembling, heart thudding against my chest, I held back no more. I could feel her all around me, drawing me deeper, pulsating, and let it all go then, experienced again that surging release, like atoms being smashed in the brain, exploding, shattering, a coming apart and the sense of annihilation and completion that follows and the drifting away.

Hours later, I became aware of a weight on me and gradually awoke. Lisette was still lying partially across me, yet the light was out. Had one of us turned it out before falling asleep? I could hear the distant hum of the forced hot water heating system and there was the faint high whisper of Lisette's breathing. Otherwise, the house was still.

What made me think of Michael? Had he been up earlier, prowling the hallways? Was he awake now?

Lisette rolled away from me. There had been covers over us, but in turning she had uncovered a shoulder. I pulled the sheet over her, and a blanket, and then quietly got out of bed. We hadn't turned down the heat before coming upstairs so it was still quite warm in the room.

I put on my bathrobe and stepped into the corridor. As I closed the door to Lisette's room I thought I heard another door close at the end of the hall, but I wasn't sure. I went into my own room and got into bed. I didn't turn on the light. I lay in the dark listening for a long time and not a sound reached me. I must have fallen asleep while straining to hear because the next thing I knew it was morning. I hadn't pulled the shades. The room was filled with light and a cardinal was singing in the peach tree beyond the window.

Mid-morning I drove Lisette to Logan and saw her onto the plane for Paris where she'd transfer to a plane for Brussels.

I'd told Michael I was going to Atlanta and then Miami while Lisette was away and that both of us would return to Brewster together. "Take care of things for us," I'd told him. He'd said that he would.

But instead of flying to Atlanta, I caught a jet to Houston. A small plane took me from Houston to Laredo. I rented a car there, an Audi, with air-conditioning, and found a motel for the first night about half way from there to Point Tartar.

Each time I go to Texas I'm struck by the enormous differences between Texans and New Englanders. When I travel to Paris, or Lyon, contrasts don't impress me, but in Texas the language, the customs, the climate and the people are all foreign. I'm accepted in France. I fit in. In Texas the aborigines regard me with distrust.

When I located a place to eat supper, there was no way to get a drink with my meal. Why did I always forget that?

The stall shower in the motel where I was to spend the night was big enough to be a car-wash.

The temperature, even that early in the spring, at ten in the evening, was in the high nineties. We still had the heat on at home.

And I actually had trouble understanding what people said to me during my first hours down there. The waitress in the restaurant had such a pained expression on her face that I asked her, kindly, I thought, "Is anything wrong?" She gave me a long venomous stare, and then said, "Ahmm tarred."

Early the next morning I checked out of the motel. It was seventy-eight degrees already and the sun had only just risen. Getting to Point Tartar was no problem. Finding the Sisters of Mercy was something else.

Had no one ever heard of them, or was it information that no one would give out to strangers? "It's a Catholic home for un-wed mothers," I would explain, and blank stares would greet my query, as if I'd asked the way to the nearest whore house. Maybe they didn't allow un-wed mothers in that part of Texas.

In the end, I went to a police station. A fair-haired giant - he must have been six-foot-four - was leaning against a dusty cruiser outside. He was wearing a Stetson hat big enough to be a beach umbrella and he had boots on with spurs on them. Otherwise, he was in uniform. A badge gleamed over his left breast shirt pocket. No gun. Probably he could handle a whole truckload of illegal aliens by just moving straight ahead and swinging his arms - maybe a backward kick once in a while so those spurs could cover his rear.

I got out of my Audi and approached him. He got bigger and bigger as I came nearer, and he wasn't even standing straight at the time.

"Perhaps you can help me," I said.

He didn't speak and he didn't change position. He just stared at me.

"I'm looking for a Home run by the Sisters of Mercy. It was here in Point Tartar forty-five years ago. Is it still here?"

"Whaa ya wanna know?"

"I'm checking on the birth date of a child who came into this world here in the early nineteen forties."

"Some kin to you?"

"Very likely."

He drew himself up to his full height and crossed his arms over his yard-wide chest, still glaring at me. I felt like a kid about to get a tongue lashing.

"Early fawties wouldabin wah tom," he said.

"That's right. I was stationed near here then before going overseas."

"Don' hardly look old enough," he said. Was that supposed to be a compliment, or was it just his cop's way of doubting every word I spoke?

The radio in the cruiser came on and made noises that were totally incomprehensible to me. The officer reached inside the car and picked up the mike. He could have reached all the way across to the other window if he'd had to.

"Twenny two here," he said. "Thass ole Tully gotta hawg loose agin. Fergitit. Ten foah."

He hadn't taken his eyes off me, as if he thought I might be about to make a break for it. By then, I think, he had me down in his book as a ravisher of women, Texas women, and a damn Yankee besides. I was beginning to feel uncomfortable.

"Ya'll gossum ahdenification?" he asked.

I gave him one of my cards and I produced my driver's license. He studied each. He was able to read without moving his lips. That was a plus. But then I thought about what it said on my card - Roy Bartlett, Importer. Jesus Christ! Next thing, he'd have me down as a drug dealer.

"Officer," I said, "I'll willingly provide you with any information you wish. For my part, all I want is to know how to reach the Home where a Michael Sullivan, who claims to be a son of mine, is supposed to have been born on January 19, 1943. Will you help me?"

Maybe he wasn't as mean as he seemed. After all, it's not a bad idea to find out all you can about any stranger who comes into a small town.

He told me how to get to the Home. It was less than ten miles away. He watched me as I drove off in the direction he had indicated, then he probably went inside to check out some of the information I'd given him.

A half mile of dirt driveway led up to my destination, when I got there. It was a three-story, nearly square ark of a building in the middle of nowhere. A recent addition to the rear looked as if it might be a modern maternity ward. I parked in front and approached the main entrance. Five steps led up to a small porch. I pressed a button there and heard chimes ring inside. There was quite a long wait before the door swung open on a tall dry woman wearing slacks and an old worn sweatshirt. "Yes?" she said.

There had been no sign along the road or on the building, so I asked, "Is this the Home of the Sisters of Mercy."

"It is." There was no Texas accent here. A second woman stood a yard behind the woman who was addressing me.

"I've come to ask some questions about a child who may have been born here on January 19, 1943."

"I'm sorry," the woman said. "We cannot give out information indiscriminately."

"I understand that," I said, "but perhaps if I could speak to the person who is in charge here..."

"I am in charge," the lady said. "I'm Sister Frances." She looked to be about fifty and there was a set, hard line to her mouth which made me think that her authority was seldom, if ever, challenged.

"What I need, Sister," I said, "is more in the nature of confirmation of facts already known to me. I'm not looking for privileged information. Could you spare a few minutes of your time, please?"

She'd seen the car in which I'd arrived and she'd taken a careful look at me. "You're not from Texas, are you?"

I told her I'd come all the way from Massachusetts just in order to make certain of a few matters that went back forty-five years.

"Follow me," she said, and turned, leaving the door open for me to enter. The other lady, eyes on the floor, moved in behind me to shut the door. Then she followed us at a distance of five or six paces. Was it because I was a man? Was no woman, not even the Directress, supposed to be alone in the presence of any male?

Sister Frances led the way into a corner room. She sat down behind a wide desk and indicated a chair on the other side of the desk where I was to be seated. A tasteless plastic cross hung on the wall behind her. Filing cabinets lined one entire side of the room. Light flooded in from windows on two sides.

The second woman sat behind me against the wall.

"Exactly what is it you wish to confirm?" Sister Frances asked.

From somewhere above me came the sound of a radio playing - Mexican music, I thought. There was no other sound in the big building. Was business kind of slow? I didn't think I should ask.

"A man who says his name is Michael Sullivan has moved into my home in Brewster, Massachusetts," I said. "He claims he was born here on January 19, 1943. He says that his mother was Arlene Lamm, of Atherton, Texas. He asserts, also, that he was adopted by a family named Sullivan, from Vision, Texas. I need to know if these things are true and I hope you can help me."

There was nothing kindly in the way she looked at me. "What is your relationship to the man, Michael Sullivan?" she demanded.

"Sister," I said, "this is not an easy situation for me. I have reason to believe that I am the father. If that is the case, I have a serious wrong to atone for."

I could feel her disapproval. How could there be any uncertainty. Maybe some explanation...

"I was nineteen years old at the time," I said. "I was about to be sent overseas as a pilot. I spent one afternoon with a young woman who told me her name was Arlene Lamm. It is possible that as a result of that meeting the man known as Michael Sullivan was conceived."

"You have taken this man into your home. You have accepted him as a son."

It was a statement, a cold statement of fact, not a question, but I felt she wanted an answer.

"Yes," I said, "I've taken him into my home, but there is still some doubt in my mind. If we are, in fact, father and son, then it seems to me there should be some bond of affection, of kinship, beginning to form between us. Instead, there is only a drawing back, a coolness, mistrust."

She offered no comment. Perhaps she was thinking I'd got what I deserved if my son refused to show me affection.

"May I see some identification?" she asked.

That caught me off balance, but I realized, then, that she was ready to tell me what I wanted to know. I gave her my driver's license and a handful of credit cards. She made a note of my full name and other information and handed everything back to me before pressing a bell on her desk. A nun, dressed as a nun, came to the door of the office.

"Would you go to the basement," Sister Frances said to her, "and get me the file on 1943."

We waited in silence until the nun returned and placed a folder on the corner of the walnut desk.

"Thank you," Sister Frances said, and opened the file. She turned pages slowly, glancing at some, reading others with care. For ten minutes she didn't look up. When she did, there was a frown on her face.

"This was all long before my time here," she said. "There is a record of a family named Sullivan - Porter T. and Ann F. Sullivan - of Vision, Texas, who adopted a male infant born to Arlene Lamm whose home was in Atherton. The date of birth was January 19, 1943."

She had hesitated. "Is there something else?" I asked.

"I'm not sure I should tell you this," she said. "Still, I don't see how it can harm anyone. If you intend to look up the Sullivans, you'll find it out anyway. They adopted two boys at the same time. I shan't tell you the name of the other mother."

I couldn't see that this information made any great difference. It was odd that Michael hadn't mentioned it. I could ask him about it. Or maybe the other child had not stayed with the Sullivans after the first year or two. Michael wouldn't even remember, perhaps. Or the other boy might have died.

"The Sullivans must have been good people," I said, "to adopt two children. My understanding is that they weren't wealthy. If they couldn't have children of their own, and wanted them, this was a generous thing to do."

Sister Frances made no comment. She got to her feet. The interview was over.

I stood up. "Thank you," I said. "You've been very helpful. I'd like to show my appreciation in some concrete way. Could I mail a check here when I get home?"

Her shoulders went back a little. "That would be very good of you," she said. "We are always in need of funds. You should make the check payable to the Sisters of Mercy, Point Tartar."

Both ladies saw me to the door. The radio upstairs had been turned off. As we went into the hallway I thought I could hear a woman crying.

Then I was outside again in the pitiless Texas sun. A hawk was turning slowly overhead and drifting northward, balancing on invisible currents, unconcerned with what went on on the earth below him.

I got into the Audi and started the motor, turned on the airconditioning and headed back to Loredo.

Somewhere in the back of my head an unpleasant thought began to stir. If the Sullivans had adopted two boys and both had grown up together, why hadn't Michael said anything about his adoptive brother? Could the other one have died in infancy, or been taken away? Wouldn't Michael have known about that, sooner or later, if it was the case? Wouldn't he have mentioned it?

There was something Michael had said about a friend who had moved away, some playmate. I remembered that when he told me that I'd felt he was being evasive. I couldn't say why. Now, and more and more when I thought about him, I was filled with uncertainty.

He'd been with us since February and had told us a few things about his life, but he never chatted on about people he'd known, or places he'd lived, or jobs he'd held. There were gaps of years and years in his life of which he had never spoken. It wasn't natural. Lisette and I were constantly filling each other in on parts of our lives the other hadn't shared. Why was Michael so different?

I'd planned to stay in Texas until I'd traced down the Sullivans and Arlene. Suddenly, I was impatient to return to the Cape, to appear out of the blue and find out what Michael was doing, maybe begin to get to know him with just the two of us in the house, because when Lisette was there he and I were not thrown together the way we would be if I went home right now.

So I made tracks back to Laredo and turned in the car and late in the afternoon I was putting my own car in the barn and walking up to the house.

Forsythia had bloomed overnight after the long cold winter and bush honeysickle had turned green, but a chill fog hung low over marshes and fields. This was already summer in Texas, but on Cape Cod spring, a teaser, was still only flirting with us.

Night was falling. I saw that lights were on in many rooms in the house. Had Michael heard me drive up? I used my key and went in the back way. Funny, how almost all Cape homes have a formal front entrance which is never used.

In the kitchen were all the usual signs that Michael had been there, had eaten something and had left everything in disarray when he was through.

The dining room was dark. I walked through it and the living room and saw lights on in my study. But no one was there.

"Michael?" I called out.

There was no answer. I climbed the stairs. A TV was on at the end of the corridor.

"Michael?" I called again.

The TV got turned off. I walked to Michael's door and opened it. He was lying on his bed with all his clothes on, shoes too. He'd been reading the book on old Cape shipwrecks. He looked over at me. "Well," he said, "back a bit soon, aren't you?"

I hadn't given any thought to what kind of story I'd tell him about my trip, but it wasn't difficult to make something up.

"When I got to Atlanta there was word that the Miami people had had to cancel," I said. "My business in Atlanta only took a couple of hours, so I got that out of the way, spent the night, did some sight-seeing and came home. Everything all right here?"

"Shouldn't it be?"

"I mean, were you able to find everything you needed?"

"I'm a big boy now, Father."

"Yes. I suppose I need to remember that. Maybe there's a subconscious wish that you were still small. That way I'd be able to share some of your early years."

It was too late for that, though. He may have had the same thought.

I looked around his room. It was a shambles. I still had my hand on the doorknob. I let go of it, leaving the door ajar, and stepped to the only chair in the room. I pushed aside the clothes that were on it, and the newspapers, and sat down.

"You seem to be taken with shipwrecks," I said, nodding toward the book. "There were plenty of them all around the Cape, in former times. Think you might want to try to locate one?"

"Why not?"

"People have been trying for a long time."

"And some are still coming up with positive results."

"They're using very sophisticated equipment now. It's expensive, too."

"Too expensive for us?"

"Definitely. But you might get lucky, just by poking around."

He set the book on the floor beside his bed. "I don't think luck has ever favored me," he said.

"A long run of bad luck is often followed by a run of good luck."

"Are you a gambler, Father?"

"Aren't we all?"

He had two pillows under his head so that he was looking across his extended body at me. He was pulling at an ear lobe with the fingers of his right hand. "What do you mean?" he asked.

"I mean there's an element of chance in any human undertaking. You start a business, you take a chance. You get married, you're taking a chance. You decide to have a career in medicine instead of in, say, music, and much of the way it turns out will depend upon chance."

"A lot depends upon your starting position."

There was that critical note again, and the bitterness. He never moved very far from it. For a moment, I think, we had both been at ease - just two men shooting the breeze, no heavy meanings, nothing really personal, and then, like some jack-in-the-box, up pops this old hobgoblin.

"Michael, I said, "you can make a new start now. Whatever it is you decide you want to do, you have the chance now to try it out and I'll do everything I can to help you."

"You don't understand, do you, Father?"

"What? What is it I should understand?"

"No. It's too easy for you that way."

"What's too easy? What are you saying? What am I supposed to do?"

"You'll need to work that out for yourself."

"You're not playing fair," I said. "If I'm your father, and I believe that I am, then let me be a father to you. Lean on me, if you want to. Tell me what your needs are. Talk with me about what troubles you. If hunting for ancient wrecks is something you've set your heart on, then we'll see what can be done to make that possible."

He locked his fingers behind his head and looked at the ceiling. Anyone else, stretched out on a bed in that position, would have appeared relaxed. Michael didn't. I was aware of tension in him. He was pulled tight like a violin string and I could almost hear a high thin ringing in the air.

"You aren't seeing clearly," he said. "There are veils over your eyes."

"But I'm trying," I said. "Help me. Give me some clue."

He didn't answer. He got off the bed and left the room. He went into his bathroom and shut the door. I sat there waiting for him to return, but he didn't.

After a long time I got up and went downstairs. I put things away in the kitchen so that Dolores wouldn't have too much cleaning up to do in the morning. I turned out the light and went into my study. There was disorder there too. I put away several books that had been removed from the shelves and left lying about. I returned some magazines to the table where I always kept them. There was a half-eaten ham sandwich on the ladderback chair by the window. I carried it out to the kitchen and put it in the garbage container.

Back in the study, I found that my desk had been gone through, drawer by drawer. Bank records had been shuffled, neat stacks of paid bills had been tipped over. My correspondence with representatives in other countries was all out of order.

The more I looked, the more enraged I became. It wasn't that I had anything I didn't want Michael to know about. I would have been glad to show him everything in my desk, to tell him anything he wanted to know about what I was worth and where I did business and how I was getting things arranged now that it was time to start letting go.

But he had ransacked my study as if there were something hidden there. Even the cabinets under the bookshelves had been opened and gone through and left in a mess. There had been no attempt to conceal the fact that he had looked. He had turned everything inside out. It would take all night to restore order.

I thought about going upstairs and hauling him out of his room, or his bathroom, and slapping him around until he was bloody. Would he have fought me? Or would he have offered no resistance?

Perhaps he'd thought he had a whole week and had intended to put things back in order before my return. But that didn't make sense. He could never have straightened the study so I wouldn't have known. And Dolores would have seen what he'd done when she came in the next day.

I let some of my anger subside. This seemed a deliberate act, when I thought about it. He'd done this because he wanted to provoke me. But why? I was hurt and confused. "You don't understand, do you, Father?" he'd said to me when I was in his room. What was it I was supposed to understand? Did he think I was so dense I couldn't imagine the loneliness, the sense of rejection, the isolation in which he must have grown up?

Or was it love that he wanted? Something he'd never known. Not for the first time, I felt the need to hold the child he had once been, hold him in my arms in order to shield him and let him know someone cared, would do anything for him. But there was no way I could put my arms around the middle-aged man the child had become. The thought was all but repugnant to me. Michael was not lovable. He was cold and distant, perhaps evil. I'd come home with the hope of finding some mutual activity that could bring us closer during the days that Lisette would remain away. It was a vain hope, I could see. He didn't want me to come closer. Maybe he wanted me out of the way.

The next morning, when he came downstairs, I called him into my study. He stood in the doorway, barely a foot into the room, impassive, his unconcern a form of insolence that made me want to stand up and strike him.

"Michael," I said, "if there is anything you want to know about my affairs, my estate, or my activities, you are free to ask me. I will tell you anything you want to know. But I do not want you, ever again, to open any cabinet in this room, or any drawer in my desk. Do you understand?"

He made no reply. He simply turned around and went to the kitchen where Dolores had prepared his breakfast. I was furious, but somehow managed not to blow up. I went back to putting things in order and by noon had finished. Perhaps there had even been some good in it because I found many things I could throw away, records I'd never have to refer to again, accounts that had long since been closed, correspondence with firms which no longer existed. It was a kind of spring cleaning I'd done and it put me in a better mood, though my anger continued to simmer below the surface.

During the remaining days of Lisette's absence, Michael and I scarcely spoke to each other. He never left the house unless someone made him. For the most part, he stayed in his own room. I heard his television going in there quite often. He took all the newspapers with him each time he went upstairs after eating. Dolores told me she was not going to clean his room any longer. I could tell, though, that this pained her because she could hardly stand it to see anything left dirty or untidy. I said fine, maybe Michael would learn to keep things in better order if we didn't do anything for him, but I dreaded to look into his quarters. If we started seeing rodents and roaches we'd have to go in and shovel out his lair. Maybe I'd throw him out at the same time.

I drove up to Boston and met Lisette when she arrived. She was tired, but filled with optimism. Her group had been able to agree on steps they could take to promote greater awareness of the need to make decisions of the World Court binding upon all members. It wasn't much, but it was a step in the right direction.

We went to an Italian restaurant in the North End, since it was suppertime, and had a leisurely meal of *tortellini* and veal cutlets and green salad. We drank half a flask of Chianti and enjoyed a dessert of *mille foglie* and were happy just being together.

She looked lovely. Her hair had been cut shorter than usual so that her small ears and long, graceful neck were more in evidence. She'd bought a new blouse, salmon-colored, with a low neckline. A waiter tended to our every need and cocked his head whenever we spoke to each other in French, convinced he was serving distinguished European nobility. Wasn't he?

We got a little high, with all the wine, and we asked for a glass of *vin santo*, after coffee, before we left. Ours was a meeting of lovers. I hoped we could keep our marriage that fresh. We'd succeeded so far.

On the drive back to the Cape, I told Lisette about my trip to Texas. She hadn't known I was going.

"Are you still that suspicious about Michael?" she asked.

"He troubles me. He's strange."

"I think you let a lurking sense of guilt seek out reasons for not believing him."

That was the kind of observation she often made - a sharp look into subconscious motivation. I'd learned to pay attention when she did that. "That makes sense," I said, "but it doesn't answer a lot of questions."

"Such as?"

"Why has he never mentioned that another boy was adopted at the same time he was? He told us he grew up without companions."

"I'll get him talking about his childhood one of these days," Lisette said. "He's much more given to talking with me than he is with you. Maybe he'll tell me something that will clear it up."

"Be sure you don't let on that you know about the other adoption. I'm not ready for him to know that I've been checking up."

"Will you go to Texas again?"

"I'm more determined than ever. I want to go to Vision, first, and ask anyone there who knew the Sullivans what the family was like and if there were two boys."

"You'll wait a while, I hope. The best part of the year is coming up now, you've told me. We'll be able to get out on the beach soon."

She loves the beaches of Cape Cod, and the dunes. We've walked many, many miles in Brewster and Truro and Provincetown before the crowds arrive and after they've gone. That year we looked forward to exploring in Chatham and to walking Sandy Neck in Barnstable. There are still places where you can be alone for hours and hours with only gulls overhead and the big sky stretching from one horizon to the other and the sound of surf on the sand when there's a wind, and the shush and whisper of small waves when the water is calm.

So I told her, Yes, I'd wait a while. I wanted to be around when she and Michael started sailing, too. I was apprehensive about that, but I didn't say so. She was looking forward to it. No need to cast a shadow over her expectations.

"There's another thing about Michael," I said, "which remains completely unexplained. He told us that he went to Atherton, Texas, eight years ago, as soon as he discovered Arlene Lamm was his natural mother. From Arlene, he found out that I was his father. Why did it take him eight years to find me? Where was he all that time? What was he doing?"

"All he had was your name, Roy, and the fact that you'd been in uniform. I doubt if the Army is in a hurry to dig up information on veterans for everyone who comes asking - especially if it sounds as if it could mean trouble for the veteran."

"Either they do give out such information, or they don't. Since he located me, either he got the information from the VA, or he found it out some other way. In either case, it shouldn't have taken eight years."

"You're turning your son into a mystery man."

"That makes him sound romantic and intriguing. Instead, I have a feeling he has something to hide. His behavior toward me is not normal. If guilt colors my way of looking at him, it's not simply because I've been feeling guilty. His manner toward me is accusatory and contemptuous. He's done nothing to show that he cares about me or about what I think of him."

I turned to her where she sat close beside me. "Be careful when you're with him," I said, on sudden impulse. "Remember not to trust him too much."

But she discounted my admonition, and I must admit that with her in the house again, the next weeks passed agreeably without any moments of serious friction. Michael was better behaved. He was less messy than he had been. He didn't open any drawers or cabinets again, except in the kitchen, and even there he began to put things away once in a while.

He and Lisette started sailing. At supper each evening they told me what progress they were making. Apparently, Michael learned quickly enough.

Lisette was delighted to get out on the water again and she took great pleasure in teaching Michael everything she knew. Michael burned and peeled and then developed a dark, ruddy complexion that was a vast improvement over his former sallow aspect. Lisette took care not to get too much sun, but she, too, tanned, and her hair turned a shade lighter.

The second week in June, I decided to go back to Texas. I told Michael I was going to San Francisco, but I told Lisette exactly where I would be, and I asked that she be in the house each evening at seven so I could phone and be certain of speaking with her. She was reluctant to deceive Michael, but agreed, in spite of herself, and on Tuesday morning I drove up to Boston and took a plane to Dallas. Getting to Vision took all the rest of the day. I found a hotel that at least had air-conditioning, phoned Lisette to tell her I'd arrived, had a lousy supper and went to bed.

Vision is a small town, not much more than a crossroads, It's in the middle of nowhere, flat country, a broiling skillet in the summer. Even in the early morning, when I got up, the temperature was over ninety.

A large glass of cold orange juice was all the breakfast I wanted. I found that in a diner. The burly matron behind the counter was frying steaks for two other customers. After she'd served them, I asked her if she'd ever known a family named Sullivan that lived in town quite a while ago. "Their first names were Porter and Ann," I said.

She looked at me out of eyes that were heavy lidded. There were gray bristles on her chin and the apron she was wearing could have covered the whole front of my rental car - a Pontiac, this time.

She said she'd heard of them, They were both dead now.

"Could you tell me where they lived?" I asked.

What was the reason I wanted to know?

"They adopted a boy and named him Michael," I said. "I'm interested in learning some more about him."

She didn't answer right away. "Are you an investigator?" she asked, at last.

"No," I said. "Just a private citizen."

"Not a reporter?"

"No. Why do you ask?"

She ignored the question and kept staring at me. She knew something about the Sullivans but was not about to tell me what it was.

"Want anything else? More juice?"

I said, "No, thank you," and she moved away. It was annoying, but I didn't think too seriously about it. I paid up and left the diner. The sun was a little higher and a whole lot hotter. I drove to a gas station. The attendant was in his forties.

I got out of the car while he was filling the tank. "Guess I'm not used to this kind of heat," I said.

"Takes a while," the man said.

"You live here all your life?"

"Just about."

I wasn't sure exactly what that meant, but I asked, "Did you ever know a family named Sullivan? Ann and Porter Sullivan?"

"Could be." he said.

"Can you tell me where they lived? I think they're both dead now, but they must have had neighbors who'd remember them."

He topped off the tank at six dollars. It hadn't taken much. A little gas dribbled down the side of the fender. That's what made it an even dollar.

"Any particular reason you want to look up the Sullivans?"

"They adopted a boy they named Michael," I said. "I'd like to learn a little more about him."

He handed me back four ones for the ten I'd given him. "Sorry, Mister," he said. "It's been a long time. Town's been changin' fast. I don't remember where that family lived. Not even sure that's the family I heard about way back when."

Another car drove up to the service island and he turned away from me. Unless I was mistaken, it was the mention of Michael that made him back off. What was going on?

Not until almost noon did I get a lead on where the Sullivans had lived. It was a street name only. No number. I parked at one end and got out of the car. My jacket was on the front seat. I'd rolled up my sleeves. How anyone could live in such heat was a mystery to me.

I didn't want to start ringing doorbells unless I had to. People would think I was a salesman if I did that. I started slowly down the street, peering at each house as if trying to recognize one I had once known, pausing, looking, shaking my head and going on. Sure enough, a lady opened her front door and asked if she could be of help. She was easily sixty, maybe more, weighed about one-ninety, and looked as if she could have gotten into the ring with Marvelous Marvin Hagler and given him a rough twelve rounds.

"A long time ago I knew a man named Porter T. Sullivan," I said. "I worked side by side with him in the fields one summer when I was going to school, before I went east. I thought I'd look him up since I'm in Texas for a couple of days."

"You got the right street, Mister, but ole Porter is daid."

"Do you know which house was his?"

She pointed up the way I was going. "It's that little ole brown one with the pink shutters. Crosbies live there now."

"Did you know Porter well, Ma'm?"

"Guess I did. Him and Ann both. Would you care to step in out of the sun, Mr...?"

"Bartlett," I said. "You're very kind. I'm not used to heat like this."

She let me in to the front parlor, from which the street was clearly visible. An air-conditioning unit was on in a back room and the temperature was a good twenty degrees lower than outside. I could breathe again and not scorch my lungs.

There was wall-to-wall carpeting. A living room "set" looked as if it had come straight out of Sears. A huge color TV occupied one whole corner. Even so, the room was comfortable. It suited its owner.

"My name is Agnes, Mr. Bartlett, Agnes Denault. Put my ole man in the ground five years ago and life's bin simpler ever since. I like to keep an eye on things. Saw you was lookin' for somethin'. Always glad to be of help."

"I appreciate that," I said.

She had put me on the sofa while she took a chair by the window.

"So you knew Porter Sullivan very well. When I knew him he was just a farm hand. He hadn't married yet. He wrote me, the only time he ever did write, when he got married, but I never met his wife. I was hoping they'd both still be here."

"You missed knowin' one of the nicest couples ever lived, Mr. Bartlett. Ole Porter never got to be anything but a farm hand, though. He was a modest man. Wouldn't step ahead of anyone else so he always just worked for wages in spite of all his talents. Why he could fix anythin', build anythin', grow anythin' any person might need. He was one in a million."

"I remember thinking the same thing," I said. "I hoped he'd find a woman as kind as he was. I guess he did, from what you say."

"Ann was the sweetest woman you could hope to meet. Always doin' somethin' for someone. Those two never had any money. You wondered how they got by. Guess it was by doin' without when it came to themselves. Even so, they managed to adopt them two boys and give 'em everythin' they needed."

"They didn't have children of their own?"

"Couldn't. First time Ann got pregnant it was in the tubes. She waited too long to find out what was wrong. Almost died. After that she couldn't ever have a child."

I was starting to feel uncomfortable. If memory served, Michael had said that Mr. Sullivan was sterile. Now Agnes Denault was telling me that Mrs. Sullivan had been rendered sterile. And Michael had led me to believe that the Sullivans were stern, unbending people, who had punished him cruelly, yet Agnes had just finished telling me they were both salt of the earth.

"Did she recover her health in every other respect?" I asked.

"Oh yes. Some ways it seemed to make her stronger. It was a great disappointment to her, of course, but she got over it. It may have hurt Porter more than her. He felt he should have got her to the hospital sooner. He was never as happy-go-lucky as he'd once bin, after that close call."

According to Michael, Mrs. Sullivan had had a bad heart and was overweight. He'd said, too, that Mr. Sullivan was diabetic as well as overweight. Agnes hadn't said anything about any of this.

"So they adopted two boys, you said."

"About two years later. Ann was crazy to have children and if she couldn't have her own she was determined to adopt some. She had the chance to get two boys at the same time. She never told me where she got them, but it must have bin from some Catholic Home. She and Porter were both devout Catholics. The boys weren't twins. They had different mothers. Different fathers, too, of course. Ann was the happiest woman in town, while the boys were small. Porter worked night and day and holidays to make ends meet. They gave those two boys more than any natural parents ever could have. Maybe they gave them too much."

"What makes you say that?"

"Well now, things just didn't work out for the best, in the long run."

"I'm sorry to hear it," I said, "I hope my friend wasn't the cause of some marital difficulty. He didn't seem like the type to wander, though."

She'd backed off from something and I wanted to keep her close to it.

"Ann was all the woman ole Porter ever needed. "Course he was a man and you can't trust a one of them." She gave me a look that as much as said - Try to deny that.

"There are some pretty good men scattered about, Mrs. Denault," I said.

"Plenty of rascals, too."

"That's true. You're right, of course."

I didn't want to argue with her. I wanted her to tell me about the boys. The trouble was, I didn't dare to ask any direct questions.

"Would you care for a glass of iced tea?" she asked. Maybe she thought she'd been a bit short with me.

"If you have some all prepared that would be wonderful."

"You set right there. I won't be a minute."

She went out and returned minutes later with a tray and two glasses of dark iced tea and a plate of cookies.

"Baked these before sun-up," she said. "I've got a sweet tooth. My one vice."

The cookies were rich and had pecans in them. I complimented her on them. The tea was even better than the cookies.

"It's hard to imagine Porter married and with children," I said. "We were just a couple of young men with all our lives before us, when we worked together that summer."

She was looking at me and listening. "You know," she said, "it's a rare thing for a man to want to look up someone from that far back in his youth. I get the feelin' that you and Porter weren't that much alike. Not even way back then. Is there somethin' you haven't bin tellin' me?"

I set down the glass of tea. I'd finished it. I'd accepted her hospitality under false pretenses and I felt bad about it.

"Mrs. Denault," I said, "you are an exceptionally perceptive woman. There is something I need to tell you. I've spent the whole morning trying to find out about the Sullivans and everyone I've met, who knew them, has become evasive the minute I started to ask questions. My interest is a very special one. At the same time, it's not an easy thing to talk about. You seem to be an understanding woman, so I'll come right out with it and tell you that I have reason to believe that I am the father of the boy who was named Michael Sullivan."

She let it all sink in. "Figgered there was more to it," she said. "So you never did know ole Porter."

"No. I never did."

"And what makes you think one of the boys he and Ann adopted coulda bin a child of yours?"

I told her. It took some time and she asked enough good questions to satisfy herself that I was telling the truth this time.

"So Michael is now livin' with you in your home in Massachusetts."

"He's been with my wife and me since February."

She crossed her arms over her formidable bosom. "You want some more tea? Maybe somethin' stronger?"

I said, "No, thank you."

She puckered her mouth for a long moment while she gazed out the window, then she said, "Michael and Jackie were two sweet babies. Like most babies. Had four of my own. All growed up and gone now. Michael, early on, showed he was goin' to be the leader. There was a lot of competitive feelin' between them. I won't say they fought from the beginnin', but they was only toddlers when you could see that Michael regarded Jackie as some kinda obstacle. Ann did everythin' she could to show them equal attention, but bad feelins was there between the two boys as soon as they was able to walk.

"They was the same age to the day and they looked a lot alike, but you could tell them apart by a kinda broodin' quiet in Michael and a real little gentleman in Jackie. I guess Jackie was just a natural victim. He was always the one to fall and get hurt. He was the one that got burned on the stove. And he was the one that died."

A truck went down the street. Mrs. Denault watched it go by. Her glass of tea, resting on a ceramic tile, rattled with the vibrations of the truck motor.

"The boys was just four years old," she said, when it was quiet again. "It was August. Ann and Porter had bought one of them rubber things you fill with water so kids can splash around in them and pretend it's a swimmin' pool. It was in their back yard.

"Ann said she was cleanin' upstairs and got through and came down to the kitchen. Michael was there with some crayons and paper at the kitchen table. She asked him where Jackie had gone. Michael said he'd gone outside. Ann looked through the window at the back yard but she didn't see Jackie. Porter had fixed a swing out there and he'd made a slide, but Jackie wasn't usin' either one. She said she looked at the rubber swimmin' pool and her heart stopped. She couldn't see him, but she knew he was in it.

"She didn't remember much after that moment. Jackie was in the pool, all right. He had his shoes on and a pair of blue and white striped shorts. He was face down in the water. Ann must've screamed when she went out there. Neighbors came around. Clem Purdy, who's gone now, pulled Jackie out and tried mouth-to-mouth resuscitation. A rescue wagon came. Jackie got took to the hospital, but he was daid.

"All that time, Michael sat at the kitchen table makin' drawin's.

"I was with Ann and Porter almost from the start. We put Ann to bed. Porter walked around like someone got his head whacked in a car accident, tears runnin' down his face, dazed. I fixed some soup after the neighbors was gone. Except for Michael, no one ate much of it.

"They was only about eighteen inches of water in that pool. No marks on the child's body. The medical report said it was death by drownin'. Accidental. Ann and Porter was the onliest ones in town believed that. Or said they did."

I was still trying to absorb it. Of course, nothing was certain. It could have been an accident. Had there been an autopsy? Perhaps Jackie had suffered a heart attack. Or had had some kind of fit. Who were his parents? Had he inherited defects that would have made him susceptible to abrupt loss of consciousness?

Another thought crossed my mind and almost got away. I was grabbing at straws, I knew, but what, after all, was there, to prove which one of the boys was my son? Maybe my child was the one to get drowned. Or was that worse?

"I'm sorry," Mrs. Denault said. "You sure I can't get you something?"

"I'll be all right," I said. "I need some time to digest all of this. I don't seem to want to believe it. What could make a child do such a thing?"

She didn't have any answer to that. Neither did I. I thanked her for asking me in and for telling me everything she had. Then I went back out into the heat.

I walked along the street and stopped in front of the brown house with the pink shutters. There were lace curtains at the windows. The yard was neat, the grass trimmed. Petunias bloomed in a flower bed along the driveway.

I could see into the back yard. There was no sign of any swing, or slide, or rubber pool - nothing to indicate that this had been the scene of a tragedy. Why should there be? It had all happened a long time ago. But no one had forgotten. Except...

What did Michael remember of it, I wondered. He'd told Lisette and me things about the Sullivans that didn't jibe with what Mrs. Denault had said. Had he recreated this family in his mind? Suppose the drowning had been an accident - two kids are playing near a pool, one slips, falls in, gets a lungful of water, the other thinks he's pretending, pushes him under again, then realizes something is wrong, escapes into the house, blocks it...

Michael had referred to a playmate who 'went away.' After Jackie's death there must have been a change in the attitude of the two Sullivans. They couldn't have gone on feeling the same way about Michael. To account for this he'd turned them into ogres, perhaps. A little boy wouldn't apply reason to such a set of circumstances. Fantasy would provide the logic - its own kind of justification.

However you looked at it, though, a child had died and another child had been present. Responsible or not, no matter how deeply buried, memory of that event would have to be carried with him. It would never go away. No doubt, it would influence everything he did for the rest of his life. A crippling burden to carry.

I returned to my car and got in, turned on the air-conditioning, and drove slowly back to the hotel where I'd spent the night. I checked out and drove to the airport where I'd rented the car. It took all the rest of the day to get to Atherton in two small planes and then a bus.

At seven o'clock, eastern daylight savings time, I called Lisette. The phone only rang once before she answered. Her voice was the sweetest sound I'd heard all day.

"Are you all right?" I asked.

"Of course, and you?"

"I'm fine. Are you in your room?"

"Yes. Why?"

"Do you know where Michael is?"

"In his room, I expect."

"Could you check on it. I don't want him to be listening in on the study phone."

She was slow to answer, but then she said, "All right."

"He's taking a shower," she said, when she came back to the phone. "What are you so worried about?"

"I've learned some things that make me quite uneasy. I spent the day in Vision. Now I'm in Atherton. I'll probably be here all day tomorrow. Please, Lisette, be very careful. Michael is not the person we've been thinking he is. It's possible that he was responsible for drowning another little boy when he was four years old. There's no telling what kind of scars that may have left in him. From the start, I had the feeling he could be dangerous. Now, I'm almost sure of it. I don't like to frighten you, but please, please, don't take any chances where Michael is concerned."

She was reluctant to believe any part of it, was sure there had been some mistake. In the end, though, she promised to be cautious. We talked a few minutes more and then said Goodbye.

Almost as soon as I'd hung up I began wondering if I shouldn't forget about Atherton and fly back to Massachusetts right away. I wish I had. I knew that Lisette had great confidence in her ability to handle almost any situation. I had never known her to be intimidated. I'd heard her sweet-talk a Boston cop out of a ticket for a moving violation. Try that one sometime. But would she know how to behave if Michael came unhinged? After what I had told her, she might alter her manner toward him. There was enough of paranoia in Michael to make him turn against her if he sensed any hint of a change in her attitude toward him.

On the other hand, they seemed to have a good, solid relationship based on their mutual interest in sailing. I had even been envious of the way they got on together. Then, too, in the months since Michael had walked up to the house in that blizzard there had never been anything to indicate that he was inclined to violence.

I put it out of my mind - at least part way out - and found where I could rent another car and checked into a motel. It was too late in the day to begin looking for the Halloway house, so I ate dinner and went to bed. But I didn't sleep well at all.

Michael had never given me the Halloway address and I hadn't wanted to ask him for it because then he would have known I was thinking about going there.

Finding the home of someone long since deceased is not always easy, but if they ever had a telephone, there is a simple thing you can do.

I found out that the district phone offices were twenty-six miles away and drove there before nine in the morning. They let me look at old directories and in minutes I found an address for Colin Halloway in Atherton in 1978. Just to be sure, I checked for 1979 and it had not been listed for that year. Michael had told me his mother was dead by then. At least that fact looked to be as he had stated it. Then I checked under previous years and found that there had been a phone under Colin's name all the way back to 1951. I didn't bother looking any farther than that.

It was after ten by the time I located the house. The sun hung in a cloudless sky like a relentless laser projector. My shirt was soaked with sweat and even the tops of my pants were moist. I'd stopped twice for something cold to drink. The sweet orange drink hadn't helped at all. And the air-conditioning in the rental car had quit.

A rusty pick-up truck was in the driveway. What may once have been a lawn was brown and dead. The graceless, two-story frame building was badly in need of paint. It didn't look as if anyone was home.

I stepped up to the front porch and rang the bell. I could hear it buzzing somewhere inside, but no one came. I knocked. I walked around to the back. A woman's cotton dress and underwear and stockings hung on a line, but there was no one anywhere in sight.

I returned to my car and sat in it, sweltering, wondering what to do next, and when I had almost decided to start knocking on doors along the street, a small red convertible appeared and parked directly in front of me.

A woman was at the wheel. She got out of the car. She was in her sixties, thin, average height, with a very determined manner. She strode up to me as I got out of my car. "What do you want?" she demanded.

"My name is Roy Bartlett," I said. "I come from Massachusetts. I believe that a Mr. Colin Halloway once lived here."

"So?"

"Mr. Halloway married a woman named Arlene Lamm. Isn't that so?"

"And if he did?"

"I met Arlene, a great many years ago."

She was looking me over as if I might be a tax collector or a repo man. Now her eyes shifted to meet mine. "How many years ago?"

"Forty-six," I said.

She took a step forward so that we were nose to nose. "You bastard," she said, and some of the saliva from her mouth sprayed onto my face. "So you're the one. Bartlett, from Massachusetts, that's what Arlene always said. God how she hated you. And now, after all these years, here you come just as if nothing had ever happened."

"A lot has happened," I said, "and Arlene had every right to hate me. You must be related to her. There's no reason why you shouldn't hate me too."

She stepped back again and took a deep breath. "What do you want?" she asked. Some of the anger had gone out of her.

"I'm trying to find out more about Arlene, and about the child she bore who seems to be my son."

The lady had herself under control by then. She was still breathing quickly, but she was clutching her handbag tightly as if to hold back the fury that was still seething within her.

"Why don't we go into the house," she said, and walked off without waiting for my answer.

I followed her. We went indoors. It was cooler inside. Shades were drawn so it was dark, too.

Although the house was plain and shabby from the outside, the interior was neat and inviting. A grand piano stood in the corner of the front room where we took seats facing each other. Waist-high bookcases held an assortment of novels and art books, a variety of plants in colored pots resting on top of them. The furniture was assorted by compatible. A floor lamp with a shade made of Degas prints of ballerinas stood between comfortable easy chairs. A good oil painting of rolling hills and low clouds hung on one of the walls.

"I'm Arlene's sister," the lady said. "Patricia Moreland. For years and years I have cursed the day Arlene ever set eyes on you. She and I, both, used to imagine what it would be like to go east and find you and break up whatever home you had with the evidence of all the trouble you caused. We never got around to it. Never had the money. And Arlene went to pieces anyway, became a hopeless drunk. Just like Dad."

She was glaring at me, the hatred still simmering, but some of the worst of it spent by now. She had made me into a monster before she met me. I could see how being face to face with the real person was causing her to adjust the image.

"You destroyed my sister, Mr. Bartlett. You ruined her life. She's dead now. Maybe you knew that."

"If my information is correct, she died eight years ago. Is that right?"

"It is. And how did you find that out?"

"A man who calls himself Michael Sullivan came to my home in February. He's been with my wife and me ever since. He told me that he'd seen his mother, Arlene, eight years earlier. He said he was my son. He said that Arlene died when her car went into the river here in Atherton, eight years ago."

"Is that all he told you?"

"He said he stayed here about a week, that his mother was an alcoholic, that she'd married a man named Halloway who was some kind of prospector, that they'd had no children. Halloway had died."

"This was the first you knew about having a child by Arlene?"

"In February, when Michael came to my door, he told me. That was the first time I'd ever suspected I had a child. I didn't believe it then. I still have some lingering doubts, but almost all of them are gone now."

"You say you're married, Mr. Bartlett?"

"Yes."

"Probably you have children and grandchildren now."

"No. I married, for the first time, less than two years ago. I have no children by my marriage. My wife is much younger than I. We hope it's not too late to have at least one child."

She took a deep breath and let it out like a sigh. It was as if she'd been pondering something and had just come to a decision.

"Arlene did have a child," she said. "She swore to me that you were the only man she had any contact with until several years later, when the child would have been four or five years old."

"Is that when she married Halloway?"

"That's right."

"What sort of man was he?"

"He was a last resort kind of man. Arlene was as pretty as a picture. She should have been able to get any man she wanted. But everyone knew she'd had an illegitimate child. In a community like this one, way back then, that was enough to spoil her chances.

"Halloway was a rough sort. He'd spent his life in all kinds of remote places. Alone. Never eating right. Half his life he never slept in a bed. He was old, too. But he had some money and he'd settled down. He asked Arlene to marry him and she grabbed the opportunity."

"Was she happy with him?"

"She was miserable. He wasn't any good as a man. He married her because he needed a nurse. For five years she took care of him while his health slowly deteriorated. He was a heavy drinker. She began drinking with him, but that runs in the family anyway. By the time he died, she was an incurable alcoholic. She gave up on life. She let herself go. She had this house and a small annuity that Colin bought for her in a moment of lucidity. She did her damned best to drink herself to death, lived in a hazy state of semi-stupefied indifference.

"I came to see her as often as I could. Tried to straighten her out. It was like trying to stop the Texas sun from beating down on you. Any time she started to sober up, she became suicidal. It was safer to let her stay drunk. And she'd been such a lovely young woman. She was the one that got the looks, the brains too. You want to see some photographs I've kept of her?"

I didn't think I wanted to, but I couldn't say No. Mrs. Moreland wanted me to see them, to punish me, perhaps, or maybe just so I'd look at her sister again as she'd once been. "I'd like that," I said.

She led me into a room at the rear of the house.

"This was Arlene's room for all the years she lived here. I don't think she hardly ever slept with old Colin. What for? By the time Arlene died, this room was a pig sty. I tried to put it back the way it was when she first got married."

I gazed around me at a room as tidy and clean as a room can get. A quilted spread of many colors covered the double bed which had a rock maple headboard. More bookcases lined one wall. A wing chair, by the window, had a small table beside it with a lamp on it. My eyes came to rest on a marble-topped Victorian bureau. Two studio photographs in thin, dark frames were atop the marble. Both were of Arlene, the Arlene I had known for a single afternoon, forty-six years before.

I stepped to the bureau. The photograph on the left had caught her full-face, smiling, wearing a pink blouse with lace-work around the collar. The one on the right was serious, confident, head turned a bit away. She was looking into a future which she expected would be exciting and joyous.

I picked up each photo, one at a time. This was the young woman I'd taken away from the dance before she could go in, and we'd gone laughing and joking across a field and had found a place on the bank of a stream under an enormous oak tree. She was lively and lovely and had never learned to say No.

We were going to go for a swim and undressed. She thought she was being naughty, liked the idea. She was curious, too. She wanted to touch and be touched. We were still laughing. We were like children, small children, carefree and innocent. It was only a game.

Did I love her? How would I know? It was wartime. I'd never made love before. She was there. She was willing. She was a flower I picked in a field, one day, and threw away.

How heedless I'd been. Those few hours had never made any difference in my life, not yet, but they'd changed everything for her.

I set the pictures back in place. Mrs. Moreland hadn't spoken since entering the room. "She was a beautiful child," she said now.

I couldn't answer. I was all choked up and there were tears overflowing my eyes. We went back into the front room and sat down again.

"Maybe it wouldn't have made any difference," Mrs. Moreland said.

I looked at her, questioningly. I still couldn't speak.

"I mean it might have been anyone else," she said. "She would have been an easy mark for any soldier. She'd lived cooped up in a girls' school for three years until that day. What did she know about life? And anyway, she's dead now."

"Can you tell me how she died?"

"Didn't Michael tell you?"

"He said she drove her car off the road into the river. Is that what happened?"

"They found her in her car, in the river, and said she'd drowned. That much seems true. But the autopsy showed she was too drunk to have been conscious, and the water in her lungs wasn't river water."

It took a moment for that to sink in. "You mean..."

"They never proved it one way or the other. They couldn't get a confession. Michael wouldn't speak, wouldn't answer any questions, acted as if he didn't understand anything. They sent him to Tidewater - that's a place for the criminally insane.

"I saw him two times before they put him away. I was notified as soon as they found Arlene in the river. Neighbors here had seen Michael around for a week before she died. They told the police to look for him. They caught him getting on a bus for Dallas. I'd never seen him before. He wasn't a bad looking man. Arlene hadn't told me about him. I always phoned her once a week - mornings, when she wasn't too likely to be fuddled. The police wanted me to identify him and of course I couldn't, but several of the neighbors were able to. And when I let the officers into the house they found clear evidence that he'd stayed here for several days.

"Then, later on, they asked me to come to a psychiatrist's office when Michael was being examined. They wanted me to talk to him about Arlene and how she was my sister and ask him some things about how he'd found her and why. But he behaved like a zombie. There was no reaction at all.

"There's no doubt in my mind that he drowned her in her own house. In the tub, upstairs. Then he carried her to the car and drove it to the river and set her in the driver's seat and let the car roll into the water. I think the police thought so too. But they couldn't prove it and he acted crazy. So they sent him to Tidewater. They should have thrown away the key.

"I don't understand what could make a man drown his own mother, do you? Was it disgust? Did he think she was better off dead? That could have been it, don't you think?"

But I didn't think so. He'd already drowned one other person, it seemed. He'd set a pattern at age four. Had there been other victims along the way? Or was his hatred directed only at those responsible for his misfortune? I thought of Lisette, alone in the house with him, and was afraid. I got to my feet. "Could I use your phone?" I asked. "I'll have the charges reversed."

"The phone's in the hall," she said. "I'll show you where it is."

She stood near me while I spoke to the operator. I heard the phone ringing. It rang eleven times before I hung up.

"There's nobody home," I said, and realized I was thinking out loud. Of course, it was not the time of day when I'd asked Lisette to be expecting a call. Maybe she was in the yard. Or had gone shopping. If Michael had been there alone, though, wouldn't he have answered. Had they gone somewhere together?

My damp shirt had gone clammy.

I thought of putting in a call to the police in Brewster. I knew one of the men on our small town force. But I'd have to tell him why I was worried, and if my fears were groundless it would destroy any chance Michael had of being accepted in the community.

I'd warned Lisette. She was a level-headed woman. Strong too. I was probably making too much of something that was not even pertinent. After all, Michael had no reason to want to harm my wife. If there was one more person he had it in for, it was me.

I decided to try calling again in an hour or so. In the meantime, I wanted to talk to someone in this place called Tidewater. I asked Mrs. Moreland how to get there and she told me. It would be less than an hour by car.

"You've been very kind," I said, as I was leaving. "Is there anything you need?"

"I've got the house," she said. "It took three years to settle that in court, but I was the only living relative, except for Michael, and he was in an asylum. My children are all grown and gone. I've got a regular job. I don't want for anything."

I gave her my card, anyway. "If you ever do need something, I'd consider it a privilege if you'd get in touch with me."

She took the card. "When you get back to Massachusetts," she said, "I'd be glad if you'd let me know if everything's all right."

T idewater was a grim complex of brick and concrete buildings, bars at most of the windows, cement walks leading from one structure to the next. There was an iron gate I had to get through to enter the place and a guard there wanted to see my license and other papers. Then he aimed me at a low building a hundred yards away and said to ask there at the desk.

I heard a kind of wailing once, in the distance, while walking, but clearly, many of the inmates were able to make themselves useful and didn't seem dangerous in any way. Several were working around the grounds, and inside the headquarters building janitorial duties seemed to be in the hands of men well-suited to their jobs.

The guard must have phoned ahead to say I was coming. A man about five foot eleven with arms that hung to below his knees and a gorilla chest approached me. This one really looked like a crazy, but instead, he introduced himself as Doctor Gaines, and led me down a long corridor to his office.

"Make yourself comfortable," he said, as he got behind his desk.

I sat in a vinyl recliner in front of him. I dislike these chairs, wouldn't have one in my own home under any circumstances, but I was stuck with it this time.

The doctor just stared at me and said nothing more. I felt like one of his patients already.

"I'd like to know something about a man named Michael Sullivan who was released from here a few months ago," I said. "Were you familiar with him?"

I got another half minute of the look-right-through-you stare. Was this Doc some kind of seer? Did he operate on intuition? Second sight?

"What is the nature of your interest?" he asked

Jesus! Was I going to have to contend with that kind of double-talk?

It served as a warning, though. I realized that if I admitted that I was probably Michael's father I could get billed for eight years of care in this charming resort.

"I'm an acquaintance of Mrs. Patricia Moreland," I said. "Michael is probably responsible for the death of her sister, Arlene. Mrs. Moreland is now living in the house in which her sister is presumed to have been drowned. Is she in danger, now that Michael has been released?"

Doctor Gaines thought that over. He must have decided it sounded plausible.

He went to a filing cabinet in the corner of his office and dug out a folder which he studied for several minutes. He brought the folder with him when he returned to his desk.

"We have a severe problem with overcrowding here, Mr. Bartlett." (So the guard had given him my name.) "Michael Sullivan never showed any signs of being, or becoming, violent while he was under our care. He was lethargic, phlegmatic, unresponsive, but he gave no trouble whatsoever in eight years. We put him to work gardening and he performed more than adequately as long as he was asked to do routine jobs. He lacked initiative, but it seemed likely that he could reenter society and settle into a job in industry or in farm labor and support himself without being a liability. We are constantly pressed to admit more patients than we can possibly care for. The committee voted to release Michael Sullivan. He was released."

"But he'd been accused of murder."

"He was found Not Guilty."

"By reason of insanity, I suppose - that doesn't mean he was innocent."

"I know that."

"So isn't there some likelihood that he'll murder again?"

"There exists a likelihood that any one of us may commit a regrettable act in a moment of stress. We can't all be locked up."

I thought that maybe some of us should, but I didn't say it.

"Did you have any chance to spend time with Michael?" I asked.

Gaines checked the manila folder. "I interviewed Michael Sullivan four times while he was here."

"And what were your impressions, if I may ask?"

"Inconclusive," he said.

"I'm not sure I understand."

"The subject was uncooperative. He would not reply to my questions. I could elicit no response, positive or negative, to anything affecting him."

"And how did you interpret that? I mean, was he hiding something? Couldn't that have been a simple way of never committing himself so that there could be no discussion of the act that brought him to you?"

Doctor Gaines gave me another one of his long looks. "A most astute supposition," he said. "Erroneous, however."

This guy was beginning to bug me. He'd seen Michael just four times in the course of eight years. Maybe each interview had lasted an hour - or had it only been ten minutes? - and he had all the answers.

"Did you know that Michael was given up for adoption at birth?" I asked.

"That's an essential part of the record."

"Don't you think that when he found out he'd been abandoned by his mother he resented that fact?"

"In like circumstances, many children feel resentment."

"Do many, then, go looking for their mothers in order to murder them?"

"I think you are trying to suggest, Mr. Bartlett, that in the case of Michael Sullivan there is evidence of severe mental derangement."

"What I'm trying to find out, Doctor, is what, in your professional opinion, was wrong with Michael Sullivan."

He was aware of my irritation. Also, he was becoming openly contemptuous of me.

"I am a professional, Mr. Bartlett. I've been a professional for more than twenty years. I've been head psychiatrist at this institution for eleven years, next October. I'm sure that your experience with persons mentally incapacitated has been less extensive than mine. Michael Sullivan, in my professional opinion, suffered from limited retardation. He may, or may not, have murdered the woman who is supposed to have been his mother. That was never proven. It is improbable that he poses any threat to anyone unless severely provoked."

He got to his feet. My time was up.

"One more thing, Doctor," I said, before rising. "When a patient is released, is some provision made for him, or her, to report to some sort of probation officer or case worker?"

Gaines remained standing, his mouth tightly closed. A minute passed. Then, with obvious reluctance, he said, "Yes."

"And has Michael Sullivan reported in?"

"That's not my department," he said.

Maybe it was, and maybe it wasn't. I would have bet my last nickel that he knew Michael had disappeared. I hoped he was getting half as worried as I was about what Michael was doing.

I let the phone ring fifteen times but there was no answer. It was three-twenty. She could still be out shopping, or visiting, or having her hair done. Then why didn't Michael answer if he was there in the house? Maybe he wouldn't, but that didn't seem likely. And what about Dolores? She should have been there.

I was at a pay phone in the town next to Tidewater. It felt like a hundred and twenty degrees, with the door closed. Not much less when I stepped outside.

I'd left a change of clothes and my briefcase and toilet articles in the motel in Atherton. The car was supposed to be returned to the rental agency there, too, but I didn't want to waste time going back to Atherton.

A local cop told me about a man with a plane who might take me to the nearest airport.

Haslett turned out to be a fubsy little half-Mexican who would do anything if the money was right. He owned some kind of Cessna and for two hundred dollars he said he'd take me to Dallas and from there I'd be able to get a connection home.

I phoned the motel and asked them what I owed them and how much extra it would be to ship my belongings to Brewster. They told me and I said I would mail them a check for the total, plus fifty dollars, if they'd make sure everything was carefully packed.

Then I called the car rental agency and told them where I was leaving the car. I asked them to send me a bill at my Brewster address, which they already had. They had my deposit. It would probably cover the total expense.

By then Haslett was ready to go. He had his own strip in a field behind his home. I couldn't help thinking that like as not he was up to his ears in bringing in illegal aliens, or maybe grass, but he was a cheerful, loquacious, devil-be-damned type who could have been useful to me in my business, I thought, except for the fact that he might be removed from the scene at any moment.

We had to circle Dallas for half an hour before they let us land. I gave my butterball pilot his two hundred dollars. "*Hasta la vista*," he said, and was gone.

The only connection to Logan was via Chicago. There was a two hour wait before leaving. I spent a lot of it trying to get an answer on the phone. There was still no one there. Maybe the phone was out of order. I asked for operator assistance and was told everything was functioning. In the air-conditioned waiting room a chill came over me. I knew something was wrong. It took a conscious effort to keep from imagining the worst.

During the flight to Chicago I was able to doze fitfully. The plane was half empty, the seat next to mine unoccupied. But the last leg of the journey was different.

When we finally took off from Chicago, not a seat was empty and it was after ten. We flew into the night and had only been in the air a short time when the pilot announced that the entire east coast was socked in with fog. Maybe we could land in Buffalo. Minutes later he came on the intercom and said Buffalo was socked in too, but the word from Atlanta indicated possible clearing there. He altered course. Shortly after two A.M. we landed in Atlanta.

We were told to stand by. The fog was lifting in the north.

I found a phone and dialed my number once more. Still no answer. There was no longer any doubt in my mind. Lisette was in trouble. I phoned the Brewster police.

"This is officer Perkins. Who is calling, please?"

"This is Roy Bartlett," I said. "I don't know if I've ever met you. Do you know me?"

"Is that pertinent?"

"Maybe not. I'm the owner of the Bartlett place. Sergeant Elvander knows me personally. If you need confirmation of who I am you can contact him."

"He'd be home in bed at this time. Asleep."

"Look," I said. "This could be a very serious matter. I'm phoning from Atlanta because my plane can't get to the Cape area until the fog lifts. I'm extremely worried about my wife. For two days Mrs. Bartlett has been alone in our home with a man named Michael Sullivan. I now have reason to believe that Sullivan is dangerous. Could you send a car out to the house to see if anything is amiss? You have my full authorization to go through the rear door by whatever means are necessary in order to check the building."

"We'd need that in writing, Sir."

"Can you tape what I'm saying?"

"Just a moment, Sir."

I heard something being moved about and thought I heard a click.

"What was it you wanted taped, Mr. Bartlett?"

Maybe he'd hooked up a recording device, or maybe the local force didn't have one, but at least he wanted me to think he was recording what I said.

"Benny Elvander will recognize my voice," I said, "so this is your authorization to enter my home by whatever means you need in order to see what may have become of my wife, Lisette. Please don't wait until Elvander comes on duty to start looking for her. Something has happened to her. A man who calls himself Michael Sullivan has been living with us since February. I have found out that he may be very dangerous. I've been phoning my home every hour or two for twelve hours and even though my wife was expecting me to call, no one has ever answered. Also, Dolores Costa, who comes in daily to clean and cook, has not been at the house. Something is wrong. Please put someone on this immediately. I will phone you the minute I get back to the Cape."

That still wasn't enough for Perkins. "There may be some very simple explanation for this," he said. "Maybe your phone is out of order."

I was close to losing my patience. "Did you say your name was Perkins?" I asked.

There was a short pause. "That's right."

"Officer Perkins," I said, "you have been given information of a serious nature. If you do not take all possible measures to follow up on what I have told you, you will be held accountable."

"Is that a threat?"

"Let me just say this: If I get home and I've caused a fuss over nothing, I will come to the station and I will be happy to have you kick my ass in the presence of all who care to watch. You have this on tape. But if I get home and my wife has come to harm which might have been prevented, had you acted, you better be long gone. Construe that any way you wish."

I hung up and immediately regretted my stupidity. Still, there are times when there's only one way to get some people moving.

I made myself comfortable in a big chair and tried to relax. If something really was wrong at home I'd probably need to be rested in order to cope with it.

We'd been told that as soon as we had clearance we could get back on the plane. I tried to sleep. Sleep was impossible. The minute I closed my eyes, all kinds of horrors flashed before me.

I was virtually certain that Michael was mad. The doctor at Tidewater had told me almost nothing, but what he had, revealed what I'd already observed - Michael knew how to bide his time. At Tidewater he'd managed to hold everything in check - say nothing, show nothing, and wait. Evidently they'd had no choice but to release him. I understood now why he'd seemed so withdrawn all the time in Brewster, why he felt no need to tell us anything about himself. Time meant nothing to him. He was like one of those jungle cats which can crouch by the path to the water hole for hours and hours, sustained by the certainty that its prey will appear sometime and it will be ready to pounce.

But I was the object of his hunt, wasn't I? He'd waited all the way into middle age to find out who his mother was and to 'track her down.' He'd waited eight years more, while at Tidewater, in order to get turned loose and come after me. It wasn't Lisette he was after, was it?

I tried and tried to reassure myself with that thought, but a niggling doubt kept creeping in. Maybe the best way to get even with me would be by hurting Lisette. If I were to lose her, no other loss could be as great.

At three-fifteen we were told to get back on the plane. We were cleared through to New York and maybe the fog would lift at Logan while we were in the air.

It didn't. We landed at La Guardia, coming in through a murky sulfur-colored soup which looked impenetrable to me. They probably shouldn't have allowed us to land at all. We were on instruments and only when the wheels touched the runway and let out that first high squeal of torn rubber did we begin to see shapes looming around us.

No flights were leaving for Logan. All weather predictions were adverse. I located a taxi driver who was willing to take me to Cape Cod.

We haggled only briefly over the fare. I was the answer to a dream for him. He might have had to wait all day at the airport, only to settle for a five-dollar fare.

He left me outside the barn. In the fog, I could only just barely make out the shape of the house.

Like a specter, Benny Elvander materialized before me. I hadn't seen the cruiser he'd parked by the road.

"Any news?" I asked.

Benny was only a pace away when he said, "Nothing yet, Roy."

"Did Perkins get you out of bed last night?"

"He sent a car out here after he got your call from Atlanta. There was no sign of anyone around the house."

"Did they force their way into the building?"

"I did. Half an hour ago. I've been through every corner of the place. There's no sign of your wife, or of the man who was living with you."

"Let's go inside and I'll double check," I said.

One pane of glass in the kitchen door had been broken

"You did this?" I asked.

Benny nodded. It was the simplest way to gain entry when a door was locked. You broke a single piece of glass, reached inside and turned the knob. If there was no glass around a door, you broke a window. It made a small noise, but if no one was home, who'd hear?

Benny followed me as I went up to Lisette's room. It only took a moment to see that everything was as usual. The only things I couldn't locate were the heavy sweater and the windbreaker she always took with her when she went sailing. My heart sank. Hadn't I warned her?

Michael's room was a worse mess than ever. I tried to remember what he wore when he went out in the boat. I thought I'd seen him in different things.

"We'll check in the barn," I said. "I think they've gone out in the sailboat."

"In this kind of fog?"

"They went yesterday. What was the weather like yesterday morning?"

"It started out sunny. Then the fog came rolling in off the water."

That happened sometimes. The water would still be cold. Warm moist air would overrun it and the fog would literally come rolling at you like some enormous cottony mass of insulation unfurling.

Before we went outside, I decided to phone Dolores. Luckily, she was home.

"Mr. Bartlett," she said. "I'm so glad to hear from you. I was worried. That Michael Sullivan called yesterday morning and said I needn't come in for several days. You were all going to be away for a while. It didn't seem right that he was calling. He's never hardly spoken to me before."

"Did he say anything about where he was going?"

"No. And that was peculiar too. You and Mrs. Bartlett always told me where you'd be if you took a trip. Is anything wrong?"

"My wife and Michael may be out on the water, Dolores. I'm very concerned. Why don't you come over and straighten things up here, and try to find someone to replace the pane of glass that's broken in the kitchen door."

"Did someone break in?"

"No. I'll tell you about that later. I'd like you to stay at the house until I can return. That way I can keep in touch with you. All right?"

"All right," she said, and we hung up.

Benny and I went out to the barn. The Blazer wasn't there. Neither were the sails.

"They're out in the boat," I said.

"Let's check that," Benny said.

He led the way to the cruiser. We got in and he made record time to the marina in spite of the fog. The kid who always took Lisette and Michael out to where the boat was moored was nowhere around. No one was going sailing today. The Blazer stood all by itself in the parking area. "You're gonna need the Coast Guard," Benny said. He got on the radio and called and handed the mike to me when the dispatcher asked for a description of the boat. I gave him all the information he needed.

"Will they be hard to find?" I asked

"Depends. Shouldn't be too difficult."

"Can you start the search right now?"

"This doesn't sound like an emergency, Sir. When the fog lifts, they'll come sailing home - if there's any wind."

"But this is an emergency," I said. "The man on board, Michael Sullivan, is believed to have drowned two other people. He's alone on the boat with my wife. I think it may be his intention to drown her, too, if he hasn't done so already."

"What'd he do? Kidnap her?"

"I don't know how he got her onto the boat, this time. Maybe he did kidnap her."

"What do you mean, 'This time'?"

"They've been going sailing together for a month or so. Just in the last two days I've found out that Michael spent eight years in a mental institution in Texas after being found Not Guilty by Reason of Insanity in the death, by drowning, of a woman presumed to have been his mother. I phoned my wife from Texas as soon as I got this information and told her to stay clear of Michael. Somehow, he must have got her to go sailing with him one more time. Now, will you please start the search?"

There was the muffled sound of a conversation on the other end of the line. Then the man came back on. "You're on a police radio from Sesuit, right?"

"Yes."

"And your name is?"

"Roy Bartlett."

"Okay, Mr. Bartlett, we'll be out to pick you up within the hour, at the marina in Sesuit. We'll want you aboard when we locate your boat. Finding it may, or may not, be easy. It depends on how many other ships are out on the Bay at this time. Our radar will pick up everything that's out there, eventually, but we can't go into every harbor and inlet. We can only cover open water, for now. Make sure you're dressed for being out in the muck for a good long stretch. Now let me speak to the officer again."

I handed the mike back to Benny. I heard him say, "That's right," a couple of times. Then he signed off.

I drove the Blazer back to the house, got together some foul weather gear and an extra sweater and came back to the marina. The fog was as thick as ever but the Coast Guard ship found its way into the harbor without difficulty.

I jumped aboard and five minutes later we were out in Cape Cod Bay and our search had begun.

LISETTE

He's mad. I know it now. I should have listened to Roy.

Roy told me that Michael had probably drowned another small boy when he was only four. What a burden of guilt for a child to carry. Unless, of course, he was able to put it out of his mind. But how does that work? Can it work? What happens to those things that are buried in some place out of reach of memory? Do they go away? Do they stay buried?

Roy said to be careful. I should have found some excuse for not coming this time.

"Let's go see if we can find them," Michael said when we heard on the radio that there were two right whales in the Bay, not far from the east end of the canal.

We'd talked about maybe getting to see whales a dozen times, but hadn't been lucky so far. I forgot all about what Roy had warned me of. We got together what we needed and drove to the marina. The tender took us out to the Sea Bird. It wasn't until we were about three miles outside the harbor and we saw the fog coming up behind us that I knew something was wrong.

"We better turn back," I said to Michael, but it was as if he couldn't hear me. He was at the tiller. He tacked right and then left again and the fog overtook us. It swallowed us and we stopped moving.

There was no wind. With the sun gone and the light only a spongy grayness around us, a chill came over me.

Michael was peering into the fog. It was as if he expected to see something there. It was not the sensible mariner's concern that another craft might come out of the murk and ram us, but the look of a man who is pursued by phantoms.

"Michael," I said softly, "if we start the motor and take a heading of south southeast, we'll get back to land."

He looked at me vacantly. We were both in the stern. Moisture was already gathering on my face and in my hair. I saw a drop of water hanging on one of Michael's ears and another on the tip of his nose.

He started the eighteen horsepower motor while I lowered the sails. Then I got out the two life jackets and put mine on and handed the second one to Michael.

"We don't need those," he said.

"We can't see where we're going," I said. "We could hit a rock or a bar or an anchored boat or a dock and get dumped overboard any minute. The water is still very cold, cold enough to finish us off if we had to be in it very long. You better put this on."

I didn't say so, but the life jacket gave me a little bit of extra warmth, too.

He let go the tiller and put on the jacket. Our heading shifted while he was at it.

The compass we had was not a very sophisticated one. We'd never needed it before. We hadn't brought any charts with us this time. The tide was falling, but I didn't remember what currents we should have expected. Besides, it wasn't at all sure how far out we'd come, or on what bearing. Only one thing was clear to me: If we set a course south we'd get back near Sesuit. The nearest land was in that direction. It was certainly fogged in by now, but even going slowly we could reach it in less than an hour.

Michael must have known that too, but when I glanced at the compass I saw that he had headed us north northwest.

"We're going the wrong direction," I said.

He shot a look at the compass. "That's all right. This will burn off soon and we'll be safer out on open water than we would be headed for land where we'd be sure to collide with something."

He hadn't looked at me while speaking. His head was turning left, then right, again and again, as he strained to see into the fog just ahead of the bow. The tension that was almost always in him had heightened. I could see the muscles in the hinge of his jawbone working in his cheek. He was grinding his teeth.

"You may be right," I said. "This fog could burn off. On the other hand, it might hang in here for a couple of days."

He had us moving at near full speed. That alone was madness. I was soaking wet already as moisture condensed on all my clothes. We'd put another mile at least between us and the shore.

"Michael," I said, "please turn us around. We can run at half speed for a couple of miles and then throttle back to the minimum for the rest of the way. That should put us ashore within an hour. And even if we run aground, or run into something, we'll be where we can walk or swim to safety. The way we're going now, we'll soon be out of gas and we'll be stuck in the middle of nowhere for God only knows how long."

But he didn't seem to hear me. Perhaps the angry sound of the motor covered the sound of my voice, or maybe there were voices within him speaking louder than anything that could reach him from the outside. I don't know exactly when full realization dawned on me, but it must have been about then that I sensed the danger I was in.

I made myself as comfortable as possible, seated with my back to the mast, so that I could watch Michael, and began trying to think of a way out of the worst fix I'd ever been in.

In the months since Michael had come to live with Roy and me I'd had the opportunity to watch Michael many times. When Roy was present, Michael kept silent unless he was asked a direct question. Alone, with me, Michael had opened up occasionally.

The first time we'd gone sailing he'd talked about dreaming of the ocean. "I never saw salt water until I came here," he said. "It was something that existed only inside my head. I had nightmares about it. I'd be walking in water up to my chin. I couldn't swim. I knew there was a shore somewhere but I couldn't see it. I'd walk a ways, pushing slowly through something warm and oily, little waves coming at me so I'd have to breathe before they covered my mouth. If the water seemed to be getting deeper, I'd turn and go in another direction. Sometimes I'd think the water was getting shallower and I'd move more quickly, but then it would rise up around me and I'd have to go back. There were moments when I'd start to put my foot down and there would be no bottom. I'd go under and start to drown. I must have had that dream a hundred times."

"But then you learned how to swim," I said.

"I did. But I still went on having that dream."

"Were you always alone in the dream?"

He'd frowned and looked at me as if I'd said something I shouldn't. "What makes you ask that?" he said.

"I don't know. I just wondered."

"Maybe I wasn't always alone," he said. "I had a feeling sometimes I was someone else, or someone else was there inside me."

He'd been seated forward, that time, and I'd been at the tiller. The wind had died. We'd been eating sandwiches. He threw a crust into the water and leaned over the side to watch it get soggy and sink. Did he see some fish take it before it went out of sight? For a split second his expression changed. He saw something, or relived something, and his eyes widened. He stopped breathing. Then he looked up at me. I didn't know how to react. I'd witnessed something I wasn't supposed to. I ducked my head and took another bite of my sandwich and pretended I'd noticed nothing. But I think Michael was not deceived.

Now, he was the one who sat at the stern and controlled where we went. Would he let me simply take the tiller out of his hands and turn the boat around? Often I had assumed command like that and he had not resisted. I sensed that there had been many years of conditioning to do as he was told, perhaps from infancy when the Sullivans had taught him what was expected of him.

But there was another element too, and that was what gave me pause. A few times I'd seen him decide he'd have his way and on those occasions there had been nothing anyone could do to change his mind. This looked like that kind of time.

Water dripped from the rigging above me and a steady stream ran down the mast against which I was leaning, got under my collar and trickled down my back. I began to shiver. The light grew dimmer as fog thickened all over the Bay.

"If you set a more westerly course," I suggested, "we might make it to near the canal and have a chance of seeing the whales."

Michael looked up at me, when I spoke. For a time, he didn't seem to remember I was there. I'd startled him. He'd been thinking of something else. I could feel him shaking the cobwebs out of his head and returning to the present.

"Maybe so," he said, and glanced at the compass. I couldn't see it from where I sat, but I felt us turn and hoped it was enough so that we'd go aground somewhere off Sandwich before we ran out of gas. Had he set the throttle back a ways we might have had gas for a longer trip, but with the way he was traveling at full speed we'd run out in only an hour or so, and if anything got in our way we'd smash into it and founder.

By now I had almost no way to tell where we were, except that we were somewhere out toward the center of Cape Cod Bay. That's where he wanted us, I was virtually certain, and there was only one reason I could think of for his wanting us in as remote a spot as possible.

When the motor quit, Michael sat staring at it as if it had betrayed him. No way could we be out of gas so soon.

"What's wrong?" he said aloud, and then turned to look at me.

I don't understand motors, or anything mechanical. Once, Roy tried to explain a few things about what might go wrong with the Blazer so that if it ever broke down I wouldn't be helpless, but whatever he told me, I'd forgotten.

"I don't know," I said. "There's got to be gas left. Have you ever worked on any kind of engine?"

He was slow to reply. Then he said, "Maybe if you come here to help me we can take this thing apart and figure out what happened."

I knew I shouldn't go near him. I got to my feet and remained with my back against the mast. "I wouldn't be any help to you," I said. "Why don't you go ahead and try to fix it."

"Are you afraid of me?" he asked.

"Of course not," I said, but it wasn't true.

We stared at each other. The Sea Bird sat motionless on the water. Fog hung all around us like a giant circular curtain.

For weeks I'd been trying to reach those places in Michael which would reveal more of him to me. I'd thought there was something accessible which I might touch and which would bring him to speak with me. He had sealed parts of himself away where, probably, he no longer looked and if I'd been able to get him to talk about them I might have been able to help him, and to understand him.

Maybe it was too late now.

"You should be," he said.

"I should be afraid of you?"

"Yes."

"Why, Michael?"

He, too, was standing. We were surrounded by silence. "Because I have to kill you," he said.

My legs felt weak. Perhaps I'd known all along that this was his intention, but to hear him say it was like hearing a sentence pronounced. Until that moment I hadn't had to believe it was possible. Now I knew.

"Have you some good reason for saying that?" I asked.

"Of course."

"What is it?"

"Don't you know?"

"No."

He shook his head. "You disappoint me," he said. "I thought you had understood."

He took one step toward me and I braced myself against the hard, solid, round surface behind me. My heart was thudding and I could feel the sweat running down my sides under my blouse. "Michael," I said, "I have something I must tell you."

He was two paces from me. He paused. "What is it?" he asked.

I took a deep breath. "I know about the little boy, the four-year-old who drowned."

He put his right hand over his mouth and his small eyes came open as I had never seen them. "What are you saying?" he asked.

"I know that when you were very young, a small boy you knew got drowned. Will you tell me about it?"

He twisted to look over his shoulder into the fog as if someone might be there watching him, or as if seeking a way to run. Then he turned back to look at me. "Michael slipped," he said.

"Did you say Michael slipped?"

"Yes. He was in the pool and he slipped and Jackie held his head under the water. They left Michael and never cared or ever knew that someone would try to drown him."

"But wasn't it Jackie who was drowned?"

"Jackie went away and Michael got out of the pool, but nobody cared that he'd been left to die."

I was confused. At the same time, I felt I'd been handed a key. Had Michael, the Michael I saw before me, been responsible for the drowning of a child named Jackie and subsequently had he blocked the knowledge of this act, turning himself into the victim and then allowing the victim to survive so that the crime was nullified?

"Were you sorry that Jackie went away?"

"Sorry? Why should I have been sorry?"

"Wasn't Jackie a friend, a playmate?"

"I don't remember."

"Would you like to remember?"

"What for?"

"Sometimes it helps to get things straight."

"I don't need any help."

"Then why do you want to hurt me?"

"I don't want to hurt you."

"But you said..."

"I have to kill you. Yes."

"But why? That's crazy."

The minute I said it I knew I had made a mistake. "Don't call me crazy," Michael said.

"I'm sorry. What I mean is that if you don't want to hurt me, you can't want to kill me."

"I never said that I wanted to kill you. I said that I have to."

"But why? I've never harmed you in any way."

"You are Roy's wife."

"And he's the one you want to harm. Is that right?"

"He's my father and he walked away from the fact of my existence. He didn't even know I existed. And didn't care."

"But he does care. From the moment you came to the door he has cared. He took you in. He'd do anything he can for you."

"He doesn't even like me."

"Michael, you don't make it easy for him to like you. If you were to show a little affection for him I'm sure he would respond in kind. He does care about you. Believe me. He wants to love you, but..."

I didn't finish the sentence because I saw him recoil. The word 'love' had made him go rigid, as if it were something to be avoided. Had he missed being loved so much he had come to hate love? Was love a disruptor? Would love make a lie of his life?

"You don't understand anything," he said. "Not one of you has ever understood a thing."

"What is it you want us to understand?" I asked. "I don't know about any of the others - except Roy, maybe - but I want to understand. Tell me. What is it I'm supposed to understand?"

He didn't reply. He stood there shaking his head as if he considered me too stupid to deserve and answer.

"I killed Arlene," he said.

"What?"

"I killed Arlene."

"Arlene was your mother, right?"

"Yes. When Mrs. Sullivan died, she left me the name of my mother. It was Arlene Lamm. I found out where Arlene lived and went to see her and I killed her."

"But why?"

"Would you do what she did?"

"What did she do?"

"She bore me and then she went away and left me. Never knew what happened to me. Never cared. She had to be punished."

There was all the singleness of purpose and the frightening lucidity of fanatical insanity in his statement.

Only a few feet separated us. Another moment and he was going to close that distance. There was nowhere I could run. Perhaps if I were to charge him I could take him by surprise. But then what?

"Turn around," he ordered.

I didn't move.

"Turn..." he started to say it again and then stopped. From somewhere in the fog came a sound - the pup, pup, pup, pup of a diesel motor. It grew louder. It was headed our way. We'd be rammed if it kept coming.

I was watching Michael. Tendons in his neck were stretched taut.

"Stop," he yelled into the fog.

His voice was shrill. It was pitched high above the low mutter of the diesel motor. Someone immediately pulled a throttle back and reversed direction. There was a churning of water close beside us and the dark outlines of a cabin cruiser took shape on our port side.

A man stood at the stern. He was barrel-chested and bald, mid-fifties, a big square face full of deep lines. As his boat drifted alongside I could see how the sun and the wind had turned his skin into something the texture of old shoe leather. His gaze went from Michael to me and back to Michael. No one had spoken.

"Our motor quit," Michael said then.

I reached over the side and held the other boat against our own. I'd be able to jump into it before Michael could stop me. The two men were staring at each other.

"You out of gas?" the stocky man asked. His voice was a subterranean rumble, not unlike the sound of the motor in his boat.

"No," Michael said. "Maybe it just overheated. I expect we'll get it started again."

"Better let me take a look at it," the man said. "If the forecasters are right, for a change, there won't be any wind to take you home for at least twenty-four hours."

He started to step over the side into the Sea Bird, but Michael said, "You really don't need to."

The man hesitated and looked my way.

"I'd appreciate your help," I said.

Our eyes locked. "Gotcha," he said, and I thought he had understood some of the urgency in my tone. "Can you hold us side by side?" he asked.

I assured him that I could.

He was standing then, as straight and solid as if he'd had both feet on a rock. There was only the slightest dip and list to our two boats in the calm, but I could imagine this man in six-foot seas in a row boat standing just as sure-footed. His eyes hadn't left mine.

"I'll get my tool kit," he said.

He stepped back down and went into his cabin. A moment later he reappeared with a metal box in his right hand. The Sea Bird rocked when he came aboard, then the man moved past Michael to the stern and set down the box.

"I'm sure I can fix it myself," Michael said.

"How long ago did it quit?" the man asked.

"Just minutes ago. Just before we heard you coming."

The man put his hand on the casing and left it there. Then he looked up at Michael. He didn't say it, but he knew Michael was lying. The metal was cold.

I could almost feel the anger coming to a boil in Michael and I saw the naked contempt the man felt for this thin person who hadn't wanted him aboard for some reason and who hadn't even known how to tell a credible lie. Had I not been there, I'm sure the man would have gone off and left Michael alone in the soup and would have hoped he would never reach land.

Instead, he flipped open his tool kit and went to work on our small motor. He was leaning to the stern, adjusting something with a long-handled screwdriver when I saw Michael lift an open-end wrench out of the tool kit, raise his arm and bring the wrench down on the back of the man's head.

I screamed as a I saw Michael raise his arm but I wasn't in time. The heavy steel wrench sank into the back of the man's skull and the sound was that of a baseball bat swung at a watermelon - a thlunk and a squish, and except for one of his legs jerking, the rest of the man never moved again. He lay draped over the outboard motor like an old burlap sack, the one leg kicking in tardy futile self-defense.

Slowly Michael turned to look at me. His face was transformed, eyes almost out of their sockets, mouth half open and the corners downturned, his neck swollen and visibly pulsing.

The wrench was still in his right hand and a long strand of something opalescent and slimy, like saliva hanging from the mouth of a bull, was slipping off the end of it, then pulling up again as if still living, and stretching thin again, nearly touching the deck.

I was using both hands to hold the Sea Bird against the side of the cruiser. I jumped into the larger craft and with all the energy I possessed I pushed the Sea Bird away from me. It was enough to throw Michael off balance.

He fell forward. The wrench dropped into the water and he hit his face on the side of the boat. He scrambled to his knees and got a hand on the bigger boat before it was out of reach. He was getting his feet under him as I turned and stepped into the cabin where the dead man had kept his tool box. There was a solid oak door on it. I closed it and locked myself in. The six-inch iron bolt would not be easy to force. Without a sledge hammer or some kind of battering ram, Michael would not be able to break in.

Two small portholes were forward. A bunk on the starboard side was big enough to sleep in. Opposite it, fishing gear hung - two heavy deep-water poles, one lighter rig, and below these something I thought might be useful. It was a harpoon head, maybe for tuna fishing. If Michael should find a way to get to me I might be able to hold him at bay with that, though the thought of using it on another human being made my insides go cold.

And while I was thinking that, I was overcome by the horror of what I had just witnessed - the gruesome, senseless murder of a powerful man whose only fault had been generosity. He'd still be alive if I hadn't urged him to help me.

The cabin cruiser rocked slightly as Michael came aboard. He tried the door to the cabin and gave it a kick. He wasn't going to be able to force it.

I heard him moving about. There was a sound he was making, almost a whimper. When he fell forward, as I pushed the Sea Bird away, I remembered that his face had struck the edge of the boat. I'd seen his mouth as he raised his head, the upper lip torn and a tooth protruding from the flap, blood beginning to flow.

So he was injured, in pain, would need medical attention. I felt no sympathy for him, however, at least not then. He was a monster. I could still see the wild look on his face when he turned toward me after crushing that man's skull. It was the look of a person completely deranged, someone who had stepped outside human boundaries and would never return.

I shuddered. I was trapped inside a tiny cabin, on a thirty-foot boat, in the middle of nowhere, in a fog so thick you couldn't see another craft at twenty feet, with a madman in control.

The motor started. Twin diesels. From one of the portholes I watched the Sea Bird fade away and vanish as we left her behind. Michael had figured out how to start the boat. No doubt he wanted to put some distance between us and the crime he had committed. What else would he be thinking?

He intended to kill me. How would he do that? How would he try? If I knew what was in his mind I'd be better prepared to thwart him, but how could anyone know what was in a mind like his? Still, there might be some logic in the way he went about things.

We were moving slowly, but I had no way of knowing in what direction. There would be a good compass on a boat like this one. Radio too. A fathometer. Would there be charts and maps? The murdered man had looked like the sort who had been out on these waters all his life and probably didn't need aids of any kind. But Michael wouldn't know where he was headed without a map. And he couldn't have known much about where we were when our motor quit either. At the very best he could only guess within several miles at where we might be.

What would the range be, on this sort of craft? If the tanks were full it could make it to Nantucket and back, perhaps. Suppose Michael tried to leave Cape Cod Bay and make a run for Boston. Could we get there? I didn't know. Anyway, what would be the point?

First, he had to get far enough from the Sea Bird so that he wouldn't be connected to it. There was a flaw in that assumption, though. He must have thought of it at the same time I did. I felt the boat turn. Was it one hundred and eighty degrees? I thought so. He was headed back. He had to find the Sea Bird and dump the body overboard with something heavy tied to it. Otherwise, anyone who happened on the boat and found the murdered man would be able to identify him. Probably he had papers on him to make that easy. So then how did he get there? The Sea Bird wasn't his. Did he have a boat? Where was it?

Michael had to get rid of the body. That was simple and obvious. Well, not so simple.

We had traveled away from the Sea Bird for not more than fifteen minutes. In fair weather we would still have been able to see her. In this fog, though, we wouldn't see her again unless we could pass within maybe twenty feet of her. And that was not going to be easy.

I was willing to bet, too, that Michael had not timed how long we'd been on the other heading. And was he holding our speed to what it had been? How about our heading now?

Insane, or not, Michael must have realized quickly that he had a difficult problem. I felt the cruiser steady and slow down. He was getting near to the spot where he assumed he had left the Sea Bird. He put our boat in neutral and we slowed further and came to rest, just barely rocking on the small waves from our wake.

He cut the motors. Was he listening? In the silence even the faint slap of a wavelet against the hull of our sailboat would give him its position. I was tempted to make a ruckus, pound on the cabin door, stomp my feet, just to keep him from hearing - if there was anything to hear. But I didn't want to provoke him. I didn't want him thinking about me. The longer he was intent on something else, the longer I had to figure out some way to escape.

Minutes passed, maybe five, maybe ten. The motors started again. At first I couldn't understand what was happening. Then I realized that Michael had decided to go in concentric circles, the tightest one possible first. It wasn't a bad plan, except that he would never be able to keep the circles from overlapping, and, of course, he had no certainty that he had started anywhere near the object of his search.

There was drift, too. In the half hour between the time we first left the Sea Bird and the time we got back somewhere near it, the current could have moved it. How far? In what direction?

For a while, Michael went cautiously, but as the circles grew wider he put on more speed. I could sense his frustration. It had become impossible for him even to tell when a circle had been completed.

He decided to alter technique and began a back-and-forth pattern starting on one side and moving forty or fifty feet inward at each turn. But of course by then he had no idea where he had started or where he was or what he was doing.

Hours passed. I'd left my watch at home and had no notion of what time it was. We'd left the house at about seven. Was it noon yet?

I was hungry. I needed to go to the bathroom. There were sandwiches on the Sea Bird. We'd never get to eat them.

I began searching the small cabin. Under the bunk bed was a pull-out drawer. It was full of charts, books on navigation, a log book of trips taken, with the owner's name on the first page - Pete C. Tully, Mashpee, Massachusetts. Every entry was in a neat square hand - date, estimated distance covered, fuel consumed, catch (if any), time of departure, time of return, weather. It was clear that Tully had labored over the writing. Probably he'd never finished high school. He was a fisherman, a commercial fisherman, and a loner. He'd been out every day that weather permitted if there was any hope of taking fish. A tally of all expenses and all amounts paid him showed he'd averaged about fourteen thousand a year over the eleven years he'd been owner of the boat.

Did he have a family? Children? Were they able to get along on just fourteen thousand a year? Alone, he might have managed, but with dependents? What did he do in the winter months?

There were star charts in the drawer. And an octant. Had he learned to navigate by the stars? Had there been trips on the open Atlantic he hadn't recorded? Vacation voyages? If there had been, they were over now. If he had a family, they would never see him again. He'd been a powerful man in apparent good health, capable, confident. I remembered the way he had looked at me and immediately understood there was something amiss, how he'd stepped aboard the Sea Bird and known how to disassemble our motor and find the trouble in only moments. Why hadn't I been able to warn him in time?

There was a small sort of bucket with a seat - a toilet? It looked as if it had never been used. Maybe it never had, until I found it in a cubby hole, forward.

Fishing gear of all sorts was carefully stored in kits and racks and all sorts of containers everywhere I looked, and nothing was loose so it could come free and rattle or shift position as the boat rocked or plunged in high seas or rough weather. I wondered if Tully had been as precise and orderly about whatever he owned in his home. Does the habit of keeping every single thing on a boat clean and in its allotted place carry over into domestic life? Are fishermen good husbands, or are they tyrants? I'd never thought about that before.

Michael, abruptly, gave up his search. I heard him cursing. I'd never heard him swear before - a steady stream of foul language. English is not rich in ways to cuss the way French is. In other circumstances I might have smiled to hear him repeating only four-letter words, but there was little to smile about, considering the spot I was in.

The boat swung onto a new course and Michael reduced our speed. I couldn't tell what heading he'd taken, but I thought it likely that he'd chosen to go north, as he had when we first got swallowed up in the fog.

It was warm in the cabin. I was thirsty. I found a jug of fresh water and a cup. There was nothing to eat, but a person can go without food for a long time when there's water to drink. I'd be able to hold out for days and days, if that became necessary.

What about Michael? He'd be cold, outside, unless there were things to wear that I hadn't seen when I came aboard in such a hurry. There had to be some foul weather gear somewhere. It wasn't in the cabin. Maybe there was a jacket on deck, too. And a lunch pail. Tully would have brought along things to eat - a thermos of coffee, no doubt, sandwiches, a thick slice of ham between two slices of Jewish rye bread, mustard and pickles - I'd better stop thinking of things like that. If such were aboard, Michael would find it. Too bad for me. But I'd manage without it. In the meantime, I'd concentrate on trying to think what Michael would do.

I tried to put myself in his shoes. He had a problem. He had to dispose of me and then save his own skin. It would be easy enough to sink the boat. That would take care of me, but it would leave him in chill deep water, no telling how far from shore. Was there some sort of inflatable dinghy aboard? I didn't know about that. Assume that there was. Would Michael have the courage to scuttle the boat and drown me and then find himself miles from land in a rubber raft barely big enough for him to sit in? Suppose the wind rose. How long would he last in even two- or three-foot seas? I doubted that he would want to try it. He had a thing about deep water, an aversion and a fascination, but I think that fear was the greater of the two. Almost every time we'd been out in the sailboat I'd noticed, just before we left shore, that he had been forced to overcome some kind of reluctance.

The fog seemed to be growing thicker. Looking through the small portholes, I could see nothing. Even the surface of the water, right next to our hull, was only a vague shifting darkness, one dimensional, fuzzy.

Perhaps it was mid-afternoon when Michael cut the motors. We lost headway and drifted to a stop and sat there barely rocking. I took down the harpoon head and held it in my hands. I stood facing the doorway, expecting Michael to try to force his way in. I waited. I was trembling.

Not a sound reached me. If Michael had been moving around I would have been aware of it. I would have been able to feel some motion under my feet as the weight of his body going from one place to another caused the boat to wobble, however slightly. But there was nothing, nothing at all to indicate that he was even breathing. Minutes stretched into quarter hours. Time, like some thick ball of taffy being pulled in two directions, became an endless filament growing thinner and thinner and sagging, ready to part.

The silence was worse than any kind of action.

"Michael," I called. "Michael, what are you doing?"

But he didn't answer. "Michael, are you all right? Are you hurt? Can you hear me?"

I knew my voice had risen. There was panic in it but I couldn't control it. "Michael, let's go back. We'll get help for you. Roy can arrange so that you are cared for, as long as you don't harm me. Do you understand?"

If he heard at all, it had no effect on him. He didn't move. He didn't reply. I wondered if he was doing it on purpose, with calculated intent. Did he hear the desperation in my voice?

If he had responded, maybe I could have talked him 'round. At least there would have been human contact again. As it was, I didn't even know if he was there. He could have gone overboard while we were still moving, could have drowned, could be gone forever.

But no. He was there on deck. Only he could have cut the motors. He was testing me. He was hoping I'd open the door to the cabin so he could rush me. And if I didn't?

Slowly, I eased myself onto the bunk. I still held the harpoon head in my hands, but now I let it rest on the mattress beside me.

For what seemed like an hour the boat was completely motionless and no sound reached me except that of my own breathing. Later, I heard a plane somewhere high over the fog, then silence again.

I wondered if Michael had fallen into a trance. How could he stand out there in the wet and the cold and not shift position as one hour passed into another? They say that in madness the body acquires special capacities. Maybe Michael no longer felt cold or discomfort. Was he stronger, too? I wished I had some way to barricade the door. There was nothing in the cabin that would be of use. I could take the mattress off the bunk and lean it there where it would act as a buffer, but it wouldn't stop anyone if the door could be broken, and I realized that this would not be as difficult as I had hoped.

It was growing darker. The long, late spring afternoon was turning to evening. I took a sip of water from the jug and my stomach growled. Hunger would become a torment if I let myself think about it. Anxiety and fear were burning calories at an abnormal rate. I needed fuel to restore those energies that were being wasted.

As dark came on, I felt a torpor creeping over me. How good it would be to lie back and sleep. I was tired. Muscles ached in odd parts of me because I had held myself tense for so many hours. I let myself sink back onto the bunk, my one weapon close beside my arm, the eerie, fog-shrouded stillness a blanket drawn over me as I slipped into a drowsiness and then let go completely and slept.

How much later was it when I came to? The cabin was pitch black. Only a thin line of light lay under the bottom edge of the door. I fumbled to find the harpoon head and my fingers closed over cold iron. The boat was stirring, shifting the way one does when someone is moving around on her. Michael had turned on some lights above deck. How long had they been on? How long could the battery, or batteries, go without being recharged?

I heard something bang against the cabin wall as it was taken from the place where it had been stored. A moment later a heavy object struck the cabin door and I knew it would only take a few more blows to shatter the only barrier between me and Michael.

I jumped off the bunk bed and stood beside the door, out of line with whatever, and whoever, would come through it. For a long minute there wasn't a sound. Perhaps Michael was standing there listening, hoping no one else on the water had heard. Was anyone else within hearing? Not likely.

Then the object struck the door again and I saw the catch where the bolt was held against the wall start to pull loose.

Silence again. A longer pause. He was listening once more. But who would be out in the middle of Cape Cod Bay in the night in the fog? I could hope there might be someone somewhere within hearing, but I didn't dare to believe it was possible.

The third crashing blow smashed the central panel and I saw a part of the instrument Michael was wielding. It was the butt end of an oar. Of course. There would always be an oar - two oars? - on a boat, something with which to push off from a sand spit if one went aground or if the power failed, something with which to turn the boat around if you got caught in a creek and couldn't maneuver.

I was still gripping the iron shaft of the harpoon. It was about three feet long with a deadly barb at the tip, sharp enough to cut through fabric and penetrate flesh. I didn't know if I would be capable of using it. Even the thought of what it could do to a tuna filled me with horror. What, then, would it do to a man, a man I knew, the son of the man to whom I was married?

The butt of the oar was withdrawn and a moment later it struck the door again, but this time it passed right through and five feet of it were protruding into the cabin.

I heard Michael fall forward. He had expected that the oar would strike something solid and instead it had encountered no resistance. The energy he had put behind it had carried him forward so that he lost his footing and fell.

I dropped the harpoon and grabbed the oar and pulled it into the cabin. It just barely fit. I crouched by the door and saw Michael through the splintered opening as he got back to his feet.

The light was on him. His face was unrecognizable. There was dried blood in his thin hair and all over his face and down the front of his shirt. The gash on his upper lip started just under the left nostril and extended for three inches along the line of his upper teeth, the entire flap of flesh hanging free and his incisors sticking through the opening. Fresh blood was flowing there as if he had just struck the same wound again.

He was sobbing - pain and frustration and madness mingling. Had there been any vestige of humanity remaining in him, had he crumpled or put his hands over his face in any sign of despair, I'm sure I would have opened what was left of the door and gone to comfort him.

Instead, he stood like some injured beast, shaking his head, blood splattering the sides of the companionway. Animal sounds came from his throat. He was hideous. Demented. Crazed.

He stepped to what remained of the door and began kicking it savagely. When it didn't yield, he used his hands and tried to tear the splintered opening wider, cutting fingers and palms.

I stood mesmerized, just inside the cabin, and saw an arm reach in through the opening and fumble to find the knob or the bolt that he knew had to be there. I could have struck at that arm. I could have picked up the harpoon and severed the hand at the wrist with that razor-sharp cruel weapon.

But I couldn't do it. I couldn't move. In the dim light that filtered around the hole in the door I saw Michael's hand find the bolt and draw it back. I saw the door swing slowly open. Michael came into the cabin, squinting, and saw where I was.

ROY

Miles Higgins was the name of the Coxwain. The engineer was named Schiffman.

Miles was just about my height, five-ten, but at least thirty years younger and twenty pounds lighter. He was one of those men who seem to be put together out of tendons and leather. Had he been a pugilist, he would never have cut. Even the short dark hair that wasn't covered by his cap had the thick wiry look of the pelt of an airdale.

Schiffman, hardly more than a kid, had a pink, girlish face and an abundance of soft flesh. Two men more different physically would have been hard to find. Both men were armed, though, and the forty-five each carried in a hip holster rode there as naturally as the belt that held it in place.

Ordinarily, I shouldn't have been aboard. Civilians aren't allowed on Coast Guard vessels. But Benny Elvander always called me Colonel, and maybe the chief at the Coast Guard station thought I was some big shot from the Air Force base when he sent the ship after me. The fact is, I stayed in the Reserve after the war ended and did wind up a full colonel.

Higgins clearly had his doubts about me, but he had his orders and wasn't about to countermand them.

Two other men were on the ship, seamen, I gathered.

"This is a twenty-five foot Wianno Senior we're looking for, right?" Higgins asked, after looking me over.

"Correct."

"And it left Susuit yesterday morning before the fog rolled in."

It wasn't really a question. He was just getting his facts confirmed.

"Two people were aboard. One male. One female."

"That's right," I said.

"The female is your wife."

"Yes."

"What about the man?"

"The man is forty-five years old. He spent eight years in a mental institution in Texas, having been found Not Guilty, by reason of insanity, in the death of a woman who was probably his mother." I didn't see any reason to say that Michael was also my son, if indeed he was.

"How come your wife was out sailing with a guy like that?"

"The man's name is Michael Sullivan. He's been living with us for several months."

We were headed out into the bay. The seaman operating the radar was standing to the right of Higgins, his face in the rubber shield around the screen. The set had a range of about thirty miles and in the dead calm around us it might have picked up the Sea Bird even at the limits of its range.

Higgins gave me one scornful look. "Why?" he asked.

So I told him. "Michael Sullivan, unless I'm mistaken, is a son of mine whose existence I never knew of until he appeared at our door last winter."

Higgins let that sink in. Maybe he thought he'd heard enough. Then he asked, "Is Sullivan armed?"

"I don't think so," I said. "He drowns people. He doesn't shoot them."

I was thinking how Lisette had been alone with Michael on the water for a day and a half already. Was she still alive? I wanted to hope that they had simply got becalmed in the fog and were waiting somewhere for the fog to lift and the wind to come up. Maybe they'd been unable to start the small outboard motor, or hadn't wanted to use it when they couldn't see ten feet in front of them. They'd be sitting out there, not knowing where they were, finishing off some sandwiches and a thermos of iced tea, tired and cold and wet. But safe.

It didn't work. Under normal circumstances they would have found their way back to land by now. Of course they might have come in and been hung up on a sand bar, aground but still surrounded by water. I liked that idea, but too many others were easier to believe: They'd hit something and foundered, they'd lost their way and headed into the open Atlantic, they'd crashed into a jetty and drowned. And the big fear, that loomed more real each hour: That Michael, by now, had added one more victim to his list.

"Has the word gone out," I asked, "to be looking for the Sea Bird in all the harbors and marinas around the bay?"

Higgins almost didn't bother to answer. I realized that someone must have been on the radio alerting every place that could be reached.

"We did that before we came out to get you," he said.

I decided I better not ask any more dumb questions for a while. It was wiser to assume that these people knew what they were doing. My anxiety, however, was not easy to control.

In addition to the three men who were in the cabin with me, there was a seaman on the bow. Most of the time we couldn't even see him, but occasionally, in a swirl of fog, we'd glimpse him crouched out there, watching the water for half-submerged logs or anything else that might damage the hull if we ran over it. I didn't envy him. He had to be soaked through, even in his foul weather gear, and cold too.

Time dragged. We didn't seem to be moving very fast. I couldn't make out what sort of plan Higgins had for locating the Sea Bird and didn't think I should ask about it. At least one hour had passed when the radar man said, "Something on the screen at 039 degrees."

Higgins swung onto the new heading. "How far?" he asked.

"Seven point four miles."

"How does it look?"

"It's coming clearer now. It's not moving."

Minutes ticked away. I couldn't help peering into the fog ahead of us even though there was no way I could see anything beyond the bow of the boat.

"Six miles," the radar man said. "Better give me about four degrees to port."

Higgins lifted the radio mike and called the base. "We've contacted what may be the subject," he said. He gave the coordinates, reading them off the loran. "We are now less than six miles south of her."

The radar operator had us alter course slightly two more times. At one mile he said, "That looks good."

Gradually the coxwain eased back on the throttle. Our warning horn had been sounding from the beginning. Any other craft should have had some kind of audio alarm too. I couldn't remember if the Sea Bird was equipped with anything of the sort. In any case, there was no answering blast.

When we were very close, the coxwain picked up a kind of bull horn and announced that this was the Coast Guard. There was no reply. I asked if I could have the horn and when it was handed to me I said, "Lisette? Michael? Are you there?"

There wasn't any answer.

The radar man said, "Two hundred feet now. Dead Ahead."

I stepped out of the cabin and crouched on the foredeck. The engineer was close behind me. I knew they didn't want me out there, but I didn't care. We could hardly see the man on the bow. He had put out fenders so we wouldn't damage the other ship when we came alongside. The only noise was the hum of the radar transmitter and the gentle swish of water along the hull subsiding as we lost headway. The low throb of the motors idling in neutral was like a heartbeat that you forgot because it was always there.

Like a gray ghost, the outline of the Sea Bird appeared before me. There was a gentle bump as we touched her. I watched as the engineer and the seaman lowered themselves onto her deck. It took less than two seconds to see there was no living soul aboard. Draped over the outboard motor, though, was the body of a man whose head had been crushed. It wasn't Michael. It wasn't anyone I had ever seen.

Higgins looked at me. "That Michael?" he asked. I shook my head.

He picked up the radio again. "We found her," he said. "Sea Bird. Out of Sesuit. No sign of the two persons who took her out, but there's a dead man aboard."

The engineer and the seaman had laid the body out on the deck so it wouldn't fall into the water. There was no doubt about death. The man's form was contorted and rigid in the position in which it had been lying for hours.

What had become of Lisette and Michael? For a couple of minutes my mind refused to function. They were gone. Were they dead too? Had both of them drowned? But where had the dead man come from?

Higgins was still on the radio. I heard him say, "No question. The man is dead...Right."

Schiffman came back on board. "He's been dead for a good twelve hours. Maybe more."

"Who is he?" asked the voice on the radio

Schiffman took the mike. "Male Caucasian." he said. Maybe fifty-five. Heavy set. About five-nine, but that's hard to say for sure since he's rigid in a bent over position. Weight about one-ninety. Seems to have been struck from behind with some heavy object. The whole back of his head is stove in."

"Any identification?"

"You want me to go through his pockets?"

"Affirmative."

Schiffman returned the mike to Higgins and jumped back onto the Sea Bird. I saw him pull a soiled handkerchief out of one pocket, a set of keys from another. In a hip pocket he found a billfold. He returned to the cabin and opened it in front of Higgins and me and the fourth man aboard. Several big bills were there, along with some photos, notes on the going price of cod and mackerel, and a driver's license.

"Here it is," Schiffman said. "Peter C. Tully. Date of birth - 2/19/26. Makes him sixty-one. Comes from Mashpee."

"What was he doing aboard the Sea Bird?"

"You mean, how did he get here? Good question. What he was doing, it looks like he was working on the outboard when someone clobbered him."

The radio was silent for a while. Then the voice asked, "You think it looks like murder?"

Higgins took over. "Chief," he said, "I don't know how it could be anything else. And robbery wasn't the motive either. There's almost three hundred dollars in this wallet - two hundred and ninety-three, to be exact."

I wondered if the chief was a Chief of police or if he was the Chief at the Coast Guard station. Nobody offered to tell me.

"Don't touch anything else," the voice advised. "You'll have to tow her in."

"But what about my wife?" I blurted out.

Higgins and Schiffman looked at me then. Higgins lifted the mike again. "Chief," he said. "There was a woman on the Sea Bird. She must still be out here somewhere. The man, too, Michael Sullivan. Since we found Tully's body on the Sea Bird, and he surely didn't leave Sesuit with the other two, maybe they're on his boat. The woman is in danger. Mr. Bartlett says Sullivan killed his own mother by drowning her. Can you find out what kind of boat Tully owned, if any. We should go after it first, it seems to me."

The chief didn't answer right away. Maybe he was consulting with someone else. When he did come back on he said, "All right. Continue your search as soon as you can make the Sea

Bird secure behind you. I'll get any information there is on what Tully owned and get back to you."

Schiffman and one of the seamen put a line on the Sea Bird and made it fast to the stern of the Coast Guard ship.

Tully's body lay on the deck just aft of the mast. It wasn't going anywhere on its own anymore.

By the time we were ready to get under way again, the Chief was back on the radio. "Tully owned a thirty-footer. Vickie, it's called. Twin diesels. It's at least fifteen years old. Still sound. I'll give you four hours. If you can't locate anything by then, you'll have to check in and turn over the body to local authorities. I'll let you know if anything pertinent shows up at this end before I hear from you."

Higgins acknowledged the message and put the mike back in place. He double-checked our position and made some entries in his log. Then we began the search for Vickie, a painfully slow search while my nerves gradually seemed to unravel.

The sound of the warning horn was hard to tolerate. It was harsh and incongruous in the fog-smothered bay. It went on and on, hour after hour. I began to wish I could rip the wires out of the walls and listen again to the stillness, imagining Lisette's voice coming to me from somewhere out there in the cottony gray mush we kept pushing through.

Near Billingsgate, we made contact with a small boat on the radar. As we neared it, another warning horn began rasping. This one turned out to be a Boston Whaler with a bearded old man aboard jigging for mackerel. He was loading up and didn't appreciate our intrusion. Had he seen any other boats?

Nothing.

Would he be able to find his way back to shore?

"Whadda you think?" his look said.

So we left him behind.

I realized, then, that Higgins had been circling the inside of Cape Cod Bay, staying far enough from shore so that before long our radar would have covered just about the entire area, with the exception of all places near land - harbors and inlets where, hopefully, others would have been checking to see if the thirty-footer had entered.

An hour passed. Two hours. Three. We were going to have to give up and head back. We'd come nearly half way around and were not far from Provincetown, if I understood rightly.

The light was changing and a slight swell was apparent. Sure enough, the sun appeared and a breeze came up out of the north. Almost at the same time, a new voice came over the radio. It was someone young and excited. "We have a report of a thirty-footer three miles west of P'Town headed for open water."

Higgins had already altered course. Schiffman had a chart out. He put a protractor on it and determined the heading we needed.

"Subject is manned by a single male, the voice continued. "The name on the hull begins with a V. Do you read me?"

"Affirmative," Higgins said. "We're on our way. Weather's cleared here. We should have no trouble with the intercept. Over."

The seaman who had been on the bow had come back inside. Higgins pushed the throttle ahead and we began traveling at what seemed like a very high speed to me. The Sea Bird bounced along behind us. I could see part of Tully's body now and then. I hoped we weren't going to add any more bodies to that fateful cargo.

The horn was turned off. The fog was gone. We could see for miles in every direction. On the horizon in front of us appeared a low dark shape. We were closing on it swiftly.

LISETTE

Michael stood inches from me, his arms at his sides, a stream of blood coming down the right side of his chin, two teeth showing through the rip in his upper lip. I could have reached for the harpoon but my body had turned to stone.

He looked at me. I don't know if he was seeing me. His small cloudy eyes gave no sign of recognition. It was as if he had expected to find someone else in the cabin. He seemed dazed.

If I'd picked up my weapon I could have run him through with it. The nightmare would have ended then and there. Or would it? For some reason I couldn't move, couldn't have harmed him. For what seemed like a full minute he was completely without defense, helpless, a lost child. I guess I knew that if I had struck him while in that state I would have destroyed myself too.

I saw awareness return to him. I saw his expression change. He raised his left arm up to the level of his shoulder. I still had all the time in the world to push him away, to hit him, to duck under the blow he was aiming at me, but I just stood there and waited, and he backhanded me. It was not a particularly vicious blow, but it slammed the side of my head against the door frame. There was a sound inside my head like that of a large timber splitting. I felt my legs dissolve, turn to jelly, as I slipped to the deck. I was surrounded by a velvety darkness. There was no pain for the moment. I don't know that I ever completely lost consciousness. I was only aware of lying crumpled and twisted, unable to move, unable to see anything clearly, just inside the cabin door.

Michael didn't touch me then. I heard him go clumping back out to the console. Heard the motors start. Felt the ship begin moving. Moments passed. A quarter hour. An hour. I can't say how long it was.

I was back in a cradle in Lyon being rocked gently by someone. Was it my mother? Her face came into focus before me, her face at thirty when she was all round and pink-skinned, always smiling and singing. But how could I have remembered something that far back? I was not in a cradle. I was on the boat of the man Michael had murdered and the soft throb of motors and the motion of this boat through the water was rocking me softly. Sleep tempted me. I could drop down into it and through to a safe silent place where all troubles ceased. It beckoned and I was on the point of succumbing when some sense of my danger returned.

My head began hurting then, a dark numbing ache. If I moved, it would explode inside my skull. If I could lie motionless, it would stay crouching there, waiting, and I could wait too. It might look away, in time, and I'd be able to slip behind something, get out of its sight, escape, but for now it was essential not to move, not even to open an eye in order to see where I was.

I realized I'd gone tense. With an effort of will I relaxed again, let all my muscles go slack.

I heard Michael returning. The pain disappeared. I didn't move. Michael took hold of my wrists and began dragging me out of the cabin. My head struck a step on the companionway and I almost lost consciousness for good, the pain was so great. He hoisted me onto the afterdeck. He was sweating and grunting and a strange snuffling noise came to me that must have had something to do with his butchered lip, but I still didn't dare look.

I felt his arms on my waist, could sense him straining. He was trying to lift me but he couldn't do it. I was dead weight and he wasn't strong. Then he held my wrists again and raised the upper half of my body and I knew in that moment he was going to throw me into the sea.

I'd drown. I wouldn't have a chance. Was there anything I could do?

He got one half of my body over the transom. For several minutes I remained draped there, like a wet towel. Was he looking at me? Did he know what he was doing? Then he raised my legs, my body tipped down, and I went head first into cold water.

I was under and I opened my eyes. Everything was the color of spit. My mouth was full of salt water. I held my breath. Then, as suddenly as I'd been immersed, I was at the surface again, coughing and spluttering. I still had the life jacket on and couldn't sink even if I wanted to.

I saw the boat. Vickie it was called. It was leaving me behind. Michael stood at the tiller, facing away from me. Had he thought I was dead when he dumped me overboard? He didn't look back. I didn't think to yell after him. Wouldn't it have been a mistake, anyway?

The fog was gone and the sun was shining. When had that happened? Maybe that gave me a reason for not calling out. I looked around and saw the Provincetown monument. How far away was it? How long could I last in this chill water? How serious was the blow to my head? I touched my temple and it hurt, but I didn't feel anything broken. At least I didn't think so. There was blood on my fingers, though, when I held my hand in front of me and looked.

I began swimming - paddling, I should say, with the clumsy jacket on - in the direction of P'Town. If I could keep going it would prevent hypothermia for a while. The trouble was that with all my clothes on and the jacket too, I'd be lucky to make any headway at all.

A light breeze was stirring. I thought it might carry me in the direction I had chosen. But how about the current? In what direction was it moving? I could make out a few landmarks. By watching how they lined up with the tower I saw that I was moving away from the shore in spite of my efforts. Perhaps the tide was falling. I was being carried straight out into the open Atlantic and with the breeze, the sea was rising. Small waves began to break against me. As the wind rose, and even if it remained very gentle, the height of the waves would increase. To anyone searching for me, I would be invisible behind even low crests at least half of the time.

And who would be searching for me? Did anyone know where to begin? Did anyone know I was in trouble? Only Roy could know, but he might still not have returned from Texas. And if he had, and had found me gone, and the Sea Bird too, and Michael, what could he do?

I almost gave up then. It seemed hopeless. If I stopped paddling, I'd conserve energy but the cold would overtake me and I could already scarcely feel where my feet were, they were that numb. If I kept on paddling and still going backwards, I'd reach exhaustion sometime and have no reserves to draw on.

How many hours of daylight remained? I couldn't tell. I couldn't remember or estimate how many hours I'd lain on the floor of the cabin. It had been nighttime when Michael struck me. Now the sun seemed to be high in the sky. If it was still near midday, there might be fishing boats coming out of the bay since the fog was gone. Someone might see me.

I searched the horizon. I looked toward shore. Nowhere did I see anything but gray-green water and the slight chop in which I was bobbing. I was a speck in the midst of a limitless expanse. I would float on indefinitely, but long before anyone saw me I'd certainly be dead from the cold, the slow creeping narcosis of falling body temperature, loss of awareness, inability of organs to continue to function.

Then I saw the boat coming, saw the burst of spume as the bow cut into every small wave. It was traveling at high speed and another smaller craft seemed to be close behind it. In no time I could see it was a Coast Card cutter and the boat it was towing was the Sea Bird.

I began yelling with all my might and waving my arms. They didn't see or hear me. The noise of the ship's motors drowned out any noise I could make and even at four or five hundred yards I was a small object in a large sea. And they weren't looking for me.

They went past without ever imagining I might be there in the water. Were they pursuing the Vickie, thinking I might still be aboard? Would they find and overtake her? I saw them disappear over the horizon and my heart sank. Even if they could catch Michael and learn that he had thrown me into the ocean, how would they ever know where to come looking for me?

For a while I'd been so excited I'd forgotten the cold. Now I realized that my legs, from the knees down, were without sensation. The wind was coming up stronger. Waves were building. I was still drifting away from land and long low swells began to take the place of the chop I'd been in.

I wanted to cry, but told myself that would be a foolish waste of energy. I must stay alert as long as possible. Maybe the Coast Guard boat would come back. Maybe some fisherman would find me. As long as daylight lasted, I had a chance.

ROY

Schiffman had a pair of binoculars out. He was looking at the boat in front of us. As we drew closer he said, "This is it. It's the Vickie. I can make out only one person aboard. A man."

"May I look?" I asked.

Schiffman handed me the glasses. We were much closer now. I focused on the man at the wheel and saw that he resembled Michael strongly, until he turned to look over his shoulder at us. The face was unrecognizable. It couldn't be Michael. And yet...

We were near enough to use the horn. Higgins announced that we were the Coast Guard and desired to come aboard.

I could see it was Michael by then, only he had been badly injured. What could have happened? And where was Lisette?

"Cut your motors," Higgins ordered as we came alongside.

Michael turned then, to look at all of us, and he saw me. His mouth opened. There was blood on his teeth and his tongue. A vermilion trickle of spittle fell from the corner of his lips. He was hideous. I thought that I should feel pity for him, wounded and disfigured as he was, but all I saw was a mask of madness.

Instead of drawing back on the throttle, he pushed it all the way forward and began a tight turn so that from where he had been, just to our right, he went ahead and swung left and moments later was headed at us broadside.

"He's going to ram us," Schiffman said.

Higgins gave us full throttle ahead. I staggered backward as the cutter surged forward. When I recovered my balance I looked aft and saw that Michael had been turning, hoping to hit us straight on, but we'd moved past him and he crashed into the Sea Bird at an angle.

The mast toppled. I saw it go over as if in slow motion, saw Michael look up at it, saw him scream, although I could hear only the splintering of timbers and the roar of motors.

The mast fell directly on him, crushing him. Tully's body, when the Vickie rammed into the Sea Bird, was lifted off the deck into the air and came to rest beside Michael like some giant crab crouching there, ready to start picking at the meat before him.

Sea Bird's hull was impaled on the prow of the Vickie. Vickie's motors continued to churn. We were still lashed to the Sea Bird by the tow line. Higgins managed to bring us alongside the Vickie. One of the seamen leaped aboard and cut her motors. Slowly, we stopped turning and an ominous quiet began to settle over all.

Where was Lisette? I left the cabin and jumped down onto the thirty-footer. Higgins started yelling at me. I didn't even try to hear what he was saying. I stepped over the two bodies on the deck. The Vickie was tipped forward, carrying the weight of Sea Bird on her prow. Was she taking water? I didn't care. I saw the shattered door to the cabin and went through it. Lisette wasn't there. I could feel the deck turning under me, my head teetering precariously over my body. If she wasn't aboard, there was only one place left where she could be - somewhere in the waters of Cape Cod Bay.

The business end of a harpoon lay at my feet. I picked it up. Where had this come from? It must have been Tully's, I thought. I saw where some deep-water fishing gear was lashed to the wall. Something was missing. The object I held in my hands had been there where the gap was. It hadn't fallen out when the boat crashed into the Sea Bird. Someone had taken it down.

The smashed door to the cabin...The weapon...Holding it, I suddenly knew how Lisette must have stood where I was now standing, locked in and safe, until Michael broke through the door.

I glanced at the end of the harpoon. It was clean. She'd never had the chance to use it - or hadn't been able to. The oar that had splintered the door was inside the cabin. As clearly as if she had stood there telling me, I could see how she had protected herself, had been prepared to hold off the intruder, but at the last moment had not had the heart to drive it into him and he'd...What had he done?

Schiffman stood at the door. I still had the harpoon in my hands.

"She was locked in here." I said. "He broke in. He must have overpowered her somehow. He got her out of here and threw her into the sea."

"Better come out on deck," Schiffman said. I let him lead me back out. "Put that thing down," he said, "and give me a hand. "We've got to get the two bodies onto the cutter before this thing sinks."

One of the seamen was moving quickly removing different items from the Vickie. Schiffman, the other seaman and I, hoisted the stiff body of Tully off the deck and onto the cutter.

Then we turned to the body of Michael. The mast had come down across his upper body, crushing him almost flat. I couldn't look at him. Schiffman and I were able to lift the mast while the second seaman pulled the smashed and exploded remains of Michael to one side. The two of them, somehow, managed to lift what still remained onto the cutter.

For a while, my anger at what Michael had done had kept me from feeling anything for him, but the sight of the mangled remains of what had been my son - what had almost certainly been my son - now filled me with a sadness that could have destroyed me. Such a waste of a life...misbegotten, misdirected...I had to push such thoughts aside.

Higgins was on the radio when I got back inside the cabin of the cutter. When he was through he said, "There's a helicopter on the way. Also, another ship will be here within minutes to stand by these two wrecks when they go down."

"My wife..." I started to say.

"I understand. We'll try to retrace the way that we came to where we overtook the Vickie and we'll attempt to cover some of the path she took getting here. The helicopter will be looking too. If your wife is in the water, at the surface, maybe we'll be able to find her. If she's not afloat, she may never be found."

Just like that. Right between the eyes. He wasn't going to let me get my hopes up.

"She's still alive," I said. "I'd know it if she'd drowned or been murdered. We've got to find her."

He didn't believe me. No doubt he considered it wishful thinking. Maybe it was. At the same time, I sensed somehow that I would have been able to tell if Lisette was no longer of this world. There had been times, when we were on opposite sides of the ocean, that we had simultaneously known something that the other was doing or experiencing. It had happened when we were only in different parts of the house, too.

Once, I was in the attic, putting away a trunk which Lisette had not wanted in her room. I set it under a small window there and then opened it and began going through things that had belonged to my mother, things I had long ago forgotten and things I had never seen. There was a faint lingering fragrance of some kind of soap or sachet my mother used to keep in her bureau drawers. I found a hand-made lace dress, wrapped in tissue paper. It was the dress of a baby girl. I lifted it out and for an hallucinatory instant I was holding my infant mother in my hands. She was palpable and warm and her life was just at its earliest beginnings. I was overcome with emotions I couldn't define and sat there with tears streaming down my face.

Lisette ran up the stair, calling my name. She'd known.

We could feel what the other was feeling. In that moment I could feel a terrible cold all around me. "We must hurry," I said. "She's in the water, but she's growing numb."

Maybe Higgins believed me. Maybe it was just that he was a pro.

A second Coast Guard cutter was closing on us and the promised helicopter was soon going thup-thup-thup-thup-thup above us.

We cut loose from the Sea Bird. The two seamen and the engineer came back aboard just as the two wrecked boats nosed over and wheezing and gurgling and spitting sank out of sight. Debris of all sorts floated to the surface - cushions and plastic bottles and pieces of wood, dungarees, biscuits, a rubber raft. A sail, with air trapped in it, sat like a giant bubble rolling and lifting and subsiding beside us as we turned back to begin our search, leaving the other cutter there to pick up whatever it might and to mark the spot where the two boats went down.

It was just after two when we began our search. The wind was steadily rising. Visibility was good, but three-foot seas made anything floating at the surface impossible to see except on a crest. There were five of us, though, four with eyes trained to spot anything untoward. There was also the helicopter. While we traveled slowly in a straight line, attempting to guess what route Michael had followed, the helicopter, at about one hundred feet, zigzagged back and forth across our trajectory so that a swath a quarter mile in width was being covered. And from the air, the waves hid nothing if eyes were quick enough to see everything that was there.

The problem, however, was that we had no way of knowing what route Michael had taken. We only knew in what direction he was headed when we overtook him.

Also, we had no way of knowing at what point Lisette had gone over the side. It could have been way back where we found the Sea Bird, or it might have been only minutes before we spotted the Vickie. A lot of miles lay between.

As the sun dropped lower in the southwest and the wind out of the north went on rising, I could feel the numbness in my body increasing. I fought it. There is a will to live in all of us, while we are healthy, and there is a power that love gives us which can work wonders at times. Is there also some kind of strength or extra quotient of determination which we can project to others through concentration or prayer or some type of thought transference?

I wanted Lisette to hang on. "Don't give up," I kept saying to myself. Or to her. And maybe she heard me. I believe that she did.

Late in the afternoon the helicopter radioed, "We got something. A quarter mile before you at two o'clock. Looks like a person in an orange life jacket."

Higgins changed course and pushed the throttle forward. In minutes we saw what the helicopter had spotted. They were hovering over it as we came alongside.

It was Lisette. One arm half rose to wave at us. She was still alive. Schiffman and I got her aboard. We carried her below decks where it was warm. I think she was trying to say my name but it was only her lips which moved and there wasn't any sound.

I stripped all the wet clothes off her and dried her with warm towels that Schiffman brought me. Her skin was shriveled and puckered from hours and hours in salt water. An electric blanket appeared from somewhere and I wrapped it around her. Her lips were a pale blue and her hands and feet were so stiff she couldn't move them. One of the seamen appeared with a cup of steaming broth. One sip at a time she was able to get it down. Slowly, her circulation returned. Her color came back and she began to cry.

I held her on my lap and rocked her back and forth like a baby. The men left us alone and went above. We were headed for shore at maximum speed. An ambulance would be waiting for us. The worst was over. We were together again.

Logs were blazing in the fireplace. We'd reached the month of June but Lisette still wanted a fire.

"Someday I'll get over it," she said. "At least I hope so. Whenever I close my eyes I can feel the cold around me again. I was so helpless. I couldn't drown with the jacket on. I watched the shore receding and couldn't do anything about stopping the drift that was carrying me away. My arms and legs slowly lost all sensation. Maybe an amputee knows how it feels."

She was home from the hospital where she had battled pneumonia. She was well again, physically. Our lives were returning to normal, but this trial was going to leave scars for a long time, maybe forever.

"Yes. Hold me," she said.

I'd pulled the sofa closer to the fire. She was curled into my arms, legs stretched out to my right among the cushions.

"He'd lost all contact with reality." Her voice was low and still had some roughness in it in spite of all the antibiotics. "He was living in some other dimension. From the moment he turned around, after bludgeoning that man Tully, I could see that he'd stepped over the edge into a place from which he'd never return."

She'd been over it time after time. She had to relive it in order to exorcise the phantoms which continued to haunt her. I knew I must listen as she sorted out her feelings and terrors and doubts.

"Could we have prevented the whole thing?" she asked, and didn't expect me to answer. "If we had called in a psychiatrist when he first arrived here...We knew something was wrong, right from the start. If we'd gotten help, could Michael have held on to his awareness of the world? He wasn't ever good company, but he was rational, it seemed. There was no sign of incoherence. Some of those first times he and I were out in the boat he even seemed to be enjoying himself. I think I knew that he needed help. I just didn't know how badly he needed it."

"You were wonderful with him," I said. I meant it. She had known how to accept him as he was and to get him to take the initiative so that she could see more of his true nature. When he was with her, he came part way out of the cavern he'd backed into. I doubt if any professional could have gained enough of his confidence to achieve that. He would have retreated again. The way he had at Tidewater.

"You know, he said he didn't want to kill me. Until Tully came along, he was still acting in a logical manner. What I mean is, he was still going through with the program he'd laid out for himself. He had destroyed Arlene and you were supposed to be next. I was a way of getting at you. He knew that killing me would hurt you. He said he had to kill me. Not that he wanted to."

She pushed away from me so that she could sit on her knees at my side, her face still close and her sea-green eyes staring into my own.

"I felt that," she said. "A couple of times he looked at me and I could see he was puzzled. He had the look of someone doing a double-take, as if asking himself who I was. I didn't know then that he had drowned Arlene. Now I can see how he would have been bewildered. It's true, he was beginning to act differently around me. I praised him a lot for the way he was learning to handle the boat and he liked that, relished it the way any youngster would. If he was drifting into a kind of mother/child relationship, with me, some part of him anyway, and if now and then he remembered he'd drowned his mother, that would account for the perplexed look he gave me. Do you suppose I could have persuaded him to try to explain?"

There was nothing either one of us could do about it now. There would be no point in blaming ourselves for what we should have done and didn't. Lisette understood that. She needed, though, to think this through and would not leave it alone.

"I might have been able to get him started talking," she said. "He must have wanted to find out what was really driving him. He was mixed up and knew it. If I'd been capable of getting him to examine what happened when he was in that back yard with Jackie...if...I think there was something there. He told me it was Michael who slipped in the pool and Jackie held Michael under water. I remember thinking that everything was turned around when he said that. Roy, could it be that the man we knew as Michael was really the child of that other mother? Maybe your son was the one to get drowned."

The same thought had occurred to me once. In a way, it was a welcome thought. It could mean that my own child was not a murderer. I'd wanted to reject that possibility from the first. At the same time, it would mean that my offspring had never had a chance to live, that some stranger had killed him while still a small child, and that stranger had come to live with us and had nearly murdered Lisette, had brutally destroyed another man, too. Which was worse? Did I want to know?

"Is there any way to be sure?" Lisette asked. "Can we find out, now, if Michael was really Michael?"

Maybe there was a way.

We went into the study. I picked up the phone and dialed information in Texas. It took some doing but eventually I was connected with the Sisters of Mercy.

"Is this Sister Frances?" I asked.

"It is."

"This is Roy Bartlett," I said. "You were very helpful several weeks ago in a matter concerning a child presumed to be mine who was born to Arlene Lamm in 1943."

"I remember, Mr. Bartlett."

"There was another male child who was given in adoption at the same time to Porter and Ann Sullivan. The man who gave us his name as Michael Sullivan, and who lived with my wife and me for several months here on Cape Cod, has died. Doubts have arisen as to his true identity. I wonder if in the birth records, which you have on file, there might be anything to indicate which one of the individuals actually came here. Sometimes at birth an anomaly is recorded - a malformation perhaps, a birthmark. Could you check the records and let me know if, in fact, anything of the sort was noted. You can phone me back collect. I would be profoundly grateful."

I gave her my number and she said she would get back to me within the hour.

It was less than twenty minutes later that the phone rang. Sister Frances was precise and cool.

"The record on the child born to Arlene Lamm shows that there was a small mole behind the left knee," she said. "No other markings were noted on either child, nor any deformities. I would like you to send me a letter confirming receipt of this information and stating whatever conclusions you draw from it."

I promised her I would do so and hung up.

Lisette had overheard the conversation. "So it was Michael," she said. "Michael was Arlene's child. And yours. I saw that dark spot. It was almost black. It was in the hollow behind the left knee. I don't think Michael knew it was there, but I noticed it several times when he was putting up the mainsail and I was at the tiller."

Sometimes knowing the truth is as painful as remaining in ignorance. I had not liked Michael. I'd tried. I'd wanted to feel for him what most parents do, to love him, if there was any way. But he hadn't wanted my love. He'd recoiled from every movement in his direction. He'd done things deliberately to anger and offend me. All that notwithstanding, I was acutely aware of how I had failed him. He'd had reason enough to hate me.

I could half imagine how the world must have seemed skewed to a small child who realizes, without having the words to put to it, just by sensing the wrongness, that he is among strangers, people to whom he does not belong, who are not his people, however good and kind and well-intentioned they may be. He'd let us know how, without ever being told, he had simply known that the Sullivans were not his parents.

Some sense of dislocation must linger with a child who is held and nursed by his mother for a day or a week after birth and who is then given away to the care of someone different and alien. Perception and memory, which imperceptibly become duller and less reliable as we grow older, must be excruciatingly sharp during those first days in the world. Did abandonment mark Michael from the beginning?

"Roy?" Lisette said. "Roy?" Roy?"

"Sorry," I said. "A moment ago you were asking yourself what you might have done to help Michael. I've been thinking how he must have been hurt very early on and how that may have had a part in determining the course of his life."

"Doesn't everyone get hurt, now and then? Don't we survive, in most cases, without..."

"Without turning into murderers?"

"I wasn't going to go that far," Lisette said.

"But that's what happened in Michael's case."

"For my part, I think the incident in the pool was the crucial one. I suspect that what happened there was more accidental than intentional.

"Look," she said. "Try to visualize two small boys in a pool in a yard by themselves. One of them, a neighbor has said, is as sweet and docile as a child can be, and the other, the natural leader, is less likable already. Surely that one resents the extra attention his companion gets. Maybe there are times when he wants to be the other boy in order to be the recipient of all that attention...affection, too. They're playing together, roughhousing, and Jackie slips. It's strictly accidental, but Michael is thinking of himself as Jackie. Children fantasize constantly. It's Jackie, in Michael's mind, who holds Michael under water. Poor Michael. He feels sorry for himself. When the other child stops struggling, Michael goes into the house. He's imagined that Jackie has tried to drown him. Maybe he's started to believe it. When Jackie doesn't reappear, he decides that Jackie 'went away.' Isn't that what he told us?"

She fell silent and I thought about what she had said. It could have happened that way, I suppose. How much confusion would there have been in Michael's mind, however. Certainly somewhere in him he must have understood what he had done. But he'd suppressed that knowledge, or twisted it. He may have thought that whatever happened to Jackie had been deserved, and therefore Michael, the one wronged, was absolved.

The result of what happened, though, was not that Michael received more attention. Even the Sullivans, who were slow to accept the truth, must have become more distant with him so that he was twice wronged, and as he grew to manhood his resentment of those who had abandoned him turned to hatred and a determination to be avenged. His natural mother and father were the ones responsible for his unhappiness. Maybe he resolved to get even with them.

I sit here in my study, looking out the window at the yard and the pasture.

Almost a year has passed since the day when Michael came up the road in the snowstorm and stopped at the mailbox to read my name there, brushing aside the first wet clinging whiteness with a bare hand.

I can see him still, as he approached the house, then stood there in front of me when I opened the door, bare-headed and middle-aged in his thin summer coat, those narrow yellowish eyes peering at me.

What should I have done differently? Could I have given him something which would have changed the way things turned out? Would he be alive now, maybe recovering, if I had known what to say to him and how to welcome him?

There has been some light snow this year, nothing like what we had last winter, though another blizzard is always possible as the shortest days come closer.

Long ago, Dolores cleaned out the room Michael occupied for the few months he was with us. Nothing remains to remind us of his sojourn here.

Almost all his life he didn't exist for me. Now he's gone and I haven't even a photograph of him, no words in his handwriting, no clothes he once wore.

He walks here with me, however, listens in the hallways, intrudes on my conversations with Lisette. Perhaps this will change in time. Of course it will. Ghosts die the same way that people do, yet his is a stubborn ghost, one which pursues me, reminding me that life is precarious and that no one escapes from himself.

Lisette went to see the doctor today. The baby is due in late April, the twenty-eighth if all calculations are exact.

This child is wanted, has been planned for, will have all the so-called advantages.

What are its chances of happiness? What role will chance play in its life?

I hear the car, the Blazer, drive up to the barn. Lisette is home. In a moment she'll come in here, her cheeks red from the December cold. She'll be smiling. We'll hold each other. Then she'll tell me what the doctor has said.